SCARY STORIES FOR STORMY NIGHTS

by R. C. Welch
Illustrated by Bernard Custodio

Lowell House
Juvenile
Los Angeles

CONTEMPORARY BOOKS
Chicago

Library of Congress Catalog Card Number: 94-39591
ISBN: 1-56565-262-2

Publisher: Jack Artenstein
General Manager, Juvenile Division: Elizabeth D. Wood
Editorial Director: Brenda Pope-Ostrow
Director of Publishing Services: Rena Copperman
Project Editor: Barbara Schoichet
Managing Editor, Juvenile Division: Chris Hemesath
Art Director: Lisa-Theresa Lenthall
Text Design: Michele Lanci-Altomare

Manufactured in the United States of America
10 9 8 7 6 5 4

Lowell House books can be purchased at special discounts when ordered in bulk for premiums and special sales. Contact Department VH at the following address:

Lowell House Juvenile
2029 Century Park East
Suite 3290
Los Angeles, CA 90067

Table of Contents

꜀꜀ ꜀꜀ ꜀꜀

The Shape of Things

ꜱ FAR AS GLEN WAS CONCERNED, MOVING INTO
the new housing development, built in the foothills outside
of town, was a great move. He still saw all his old friends at
school, and he got to make a lot of new friends, too. The
forested hills, sparkling streams, and green meadows were
the best backyard he could have hoped for, and he and
Dolph, his two-year-old German shepherd, spent as much
time as they could exploring the unknown countryside.

Now, out with Dolph, about to embark on another
exploration, Glen reached the wooden fence that separated
the asphalt pavement from a dirt service road leading into
the hills. He wriggled through the fence, and Dolph eagerly
followed. Then, once they were safe from any traffic, Glen
took Dolph off the leash. Happy to be free, the dog raced
into the tall grass of a nearby field as Glen sauntered along
the road.

Glen had already decided that today he and Dolph
would probe deeper into a narrow canyon they had found
last weekend. The walls of the hills were so close together
and covered so thickly with brush that it looked nearly

impossible to enter the small gap. But Glen had found a narrow trail, almost invisible in the brush, and he wanted to see where it led.

Keeping an eye on Dolph to make sure he didn't wander too far, Glen conjured up images of hidden treasures and old Indian camps tucked away in the sheltered ravine. Who knew what he'd find there? Why, he might even come across an ancient civilization!

The weekend before, Glen had made sure to carefully memorize the area around the hidden entrance to the ravine, so now he easily found it once again. Whistling for Dolph to follow, he snaked his way along the faint path.

The hot afternoon sun was filtered by the ravine's leafy branches, but Glen was still sweating by the time he made it to the end of the canyon. There, the mountain walls opened slightly to form a small, box-shaped valley that was covered in thick brush and dotted here and there with gigantic oak trees. A small mound rose at the far end of the hidden hollow. On it was an old building that looked like it might have been a small house at one time. But even from where Glen stood, he could see that the roof was partially caved in, and there were only gaping holes where the windows had once been.

"Cool," Glen whispered. "Maybe it's haunted." Then, calling Dolph, he started across the valley to explore the abandoned house. Climbing from rock to rock, he made his way up the hill until he was standing right at the front door of the place. Very edgy, Dolph paced back and forth at his side, as if he smelled something suspicious.

"What is it, boy?" Glen asked. "Some kind of animal?" Glen sniffed the air himself. *He* certainly couldn't smell anything.

Taking a step closer, Glen peered into the dark doorway. He motioned for Dolph to follow, but the shepherd stood where he was and whined.

"What?" Glen asked, a little irritated at his dog's behavior. Still, Dolph swung his head back and forth and refused to come any closer to the gaping doorway.

Starting to grow worried by Dolph's reaction, Glen tentatively took another step closer, and stared into the small, one-room building. He stood as still as a statue, readying himself to run in case some wild animal came rushing out at him.

After a long moment, when nothing happened, Glen let his breath whoosh out. "Come on, you big baby," he said, glancing back at Dolph. "There's nothing in there." To prove it to himself and to his dog, Glen stepped through the open doorway.

The interior was a mess. Debris from the collapsed roof covered half the floor, which was thick with dirt and small weeds that sprouted from the moldering pile of masonry. Now Glen thought he smelled something, too— some kind of animal—and he figured that it was what his dog had smelled. *Must've been something big*, Glen thought, seeing that Dolph still refused to follow him.

Not bothering to enter any further, Glen turned and went back to his dog. "You scaredy-cat," he said, ruffling Dolph's neck. "I thought you were a dog, not a mouse." Obviously happy that Glen had come back, Dolph licked him and the two of them turned away from the hut to explore the rest of the area.

But soon Glen realized that there was not much else

of interest. So, with Dolph ranging off to one side, he turned back toward the entrance of the canyon.

He had not gone far when suddenly he saw a man enter the hidden valley. Stopping in surprise, Glen quickly stepped behind a tree and watched as the man walked directly to the abandoned ruins and went inside. Overcome with curiosity, Glen crept back toward the house.

But halfway between the canyon entrance and the doorway to the house, Glen stopped dead in his tracks. Shaking with fear, he crouched behind a large bush. Coming out of the house was an animal Glen had only seen behind bars at the zoo. It was a gray wolf—a very *large* gray wolf.

But that house was empty, his mind insisted. *I saw it myself*. And then a darker thought shadowed his brain. *What happened to the man who went inside?*

The wolf raised its muzzle and sniffed at the air. Glen's fear spread through his body. It started at his legs and moved up to clutch at his chest, making it hard to keep from screaming. His breath came faster and faster, and it was as if his fear was calling to the beast. The wolf turned its head and stared in Glen's direction. Then it lightly jumped down the rocks and disappeared into the brush.

Glen sucked in his breath and began to ease backward from his hiding place. Then his nerve broke and he jumped up and fled. His imagination racing along with him, he could almost hear the bushes snapping behind him and feel the hot breath of the wolf on his legs.

Suddenly there was a snarl, followed by a yelp and the sound of thrashing in the bushes. *Dolph!* Glen thought, skidding to a halt and looking behind him.

But Glen could see nothing, and all he could hear were the sounds of animals in combat echoing off the high canyon walls. Torn by indecision, Glen took a few steps back toward the two fighting animals. Then, with a cry of despair for his dog, he turned and ran out of the valley.

Blundering along the path, ignoring the branches that grabbed at him as he pushed along, crying and cursing, Glen fought his way through to the clear land on the outside of the ravine. Once out, he staggered to a stop and peered back at the valley he had just escaped.

"Dolph," he whispered, feeling sick at heart. He waited for a few minutes, then trudged home, making up a story to tell his parents about how Dolph had run away. He felt like such a coward that he just couldn't tell them the truth. Luckily his tears were very convincing, and his parents sent him to bed early.

Glen spent that night endlessly reliving the events of the afternoon. The image of Dolph being torn to shreds seemed to tear at Glen, and the guilt he felt for having left his faithful friend behind was practically unbearable.

But as guilty as Glen was, he was equally puzzled. Try as he might, Glen could not explain where that wolf had come from. If the man had brought it with him, Glen was sure he would have seen it. He was also sure he would have seen something as big as a wolf the first time he looked into the abandoned house if it had already been inside. Besides, if the ferocious-looking animal had been in there, Glen knew it wouldn't have let him come so close.

But either of those unlikely scenarios was far more possible than his deepest, darkest thought—that the man and the wolf were actually the same creature.

The next morning, however, the impossible suddenly became frighteningly possible when Glen overheard his dad's morning news program.

"In local news," the announcer was saying, "the body of an unidentified male was found in the Shorthorn foothills this morning by a group of hikers. Apparently the man died as a result of blood loss from wounds inflicted to his arms and neck. Doctors say the wounds closely resemble those caused by dog bites, and are cautioning residents in the area to be on the lookout for any stray dogs that are behaving oddly."

Glen couldn't hear the rest of the broadcast over the roaring in his ears from his own raging thoughts. *No! Werewolves don't exist!* his mind screamed. *The announcer just confirmed that the man I saw going into the house was just a victim of the wolf—not the wolf itself.*

Still, even if that were the case, Glen now had to answer his questions about Dolph before he went crazy with guilt. Maybe Dolph was alive and he could save him. But how? He was too scared to return to the valley alone. What if the wolf was still running loose? With no idea of what to do, Glen decided to go over to his friend Brandon's house. Maybe he would have some ideas.

As he approached his friend's two-story home at the end of the block, Glen saw Brandon coming up the sidewalk toward him. "Sorry to hear about Dolph," Brandon called as he got closer.

That's odd, Glen thought. *I haven't told anyone but my parents about Dolph.* "How did you know?" Glen called back.

Brandon ignored the question as he walked up to meet Glen. He had an excited gleam in his eye. "Did you hear about the guy they found this morning?"

"Yeah," Glen answered. "Sounds like he got attacked by a dog or something."

"I know," Brandon went on, the excitement in his eyes turning mischievous. "I'm going to go up there and have a look around. Want to come along? Maybe we could trap the dog and become heroes."

Glen smiled. His problem was solved! Now he wouldn't have to go into the canyon alone. "Yeah, sure," he said casually, feeling a twinge of guilt for not telling Brandon what had happened the day before.

꙼ꙮ꙼ ꙼ꙮ꙼ ꙼ꙮ꙼

Brandon didn't seem to have any clear idea of where to go, and Glen had no problem subtly guiding him toward the canyon entrance. As they walked along the trail, Glen noticed that it was as dark and overgrown as before, with no signs of his terrified flight through the bushes yesterday afternoon.

"I wonder where this path goes," Brandon said as he followed Glen along the trail.

"I don't know," Glen lied. "Maybe it's some kind of animal trail."

As they approached the hidden valley, Glen looked around cautiously, half-expecting the gray wolf to come leaping out at him. He tried not to let Brandon see how scared he was, but by the time they reached the open end of the canyon, even though they hadn't encountered anything more threatening than a patch of poison oak, Glen was trembling from head to toe.

"Look at that," Brandon exclaimed, too interested in the expedition to notice Glen's fear. "It's an abandoned house."

Glen glanced up at the ruins, impatient to find the site where he'd heard Dolph and the wolf fighting. Still, he had to pretend to be interested in Brandon's discovery. "Yeah," he said, trying to sound excited. "Wonder what it's doing here?"

"Come on," Brandon said, starting forward. "Let's go check it out."

Too late to turn back now, Glen thought, trying to shrug off his fear as he followed his friend.

As they neared the house, Glen angled himself toward where his dog had fought the wolf, and suddenly he saw something lying under a bush . . . something bloody. Afraid to look, Glen tried to calm his pounding heart as he stepped closer. Then, with a gasp, he saw that it was Dolph, lying in a blood-stained patch of torn-up earth. The poor dog was plainly dead, his throat ripped to shreds. When Glen saw a fat fly land on one of Dolph's still-opened eyes, he broke out crying.

"What is it?" Brandon asked as he came up behind Glen. "What's wrong?" And then he looked down. "Oh," was all he could say.

Glen tried to master his grief. "It's my dog," he said, then burst out into fresh tears.

Brandon stared at the dog's stiff body for a few

moments. "You think the same thing that killed that man killed Dolph?" he murmured.

Glen nodded. "I'm sure of it."

Brandon stared at Dolph's bloody body for a little longer, then said quietly, "Come on. Let's go."

Glen let himself be led to the ruins. *I abandoned him,* he wailed in his mind. *Dolph was protecting me and I ran away like a coward!*

Still weeping with guilt, Glen hardly noticed as he and Brandon reached the dark doorway. Brandon ducked inside first, and Glen blindly followed. Then, as if a bucket of cold water had been thrown at him, shock snapped Glen out of his depression. There, standing inside the house, were five people . . . and Brandon was standing with them. All of them—Brandon included—were staring at Glen with hatred burning in their eyes.

"What's going on?" Glen asked, looking at the boy he'd thought was his friend. "Brandon," he said, his voice rising in panic, "what's going on?"

"Your stupid dog killed one of us," Brandon answered angrily, "so we killed him. What were you doing up here in the first place, you idiot?"

"I—I don't know," Glen stammered. "Dolph and I were just exploring. If I'd known that *you* . . . that the man we met were . . ." But words failed Glen as he realized that he had no idea of any connection between Brandon and these people . . . *and* the man he had seen yesterday.

As Glen tried to figure out whether or not he should run, Brandon and the others huddled together in a corner of the dilapidated room, obviously deciding his fate. Finally the oldest of the group nodded, and Brandon produced a thermos from a pile of rubble. Unscrewing the lid, he took a long swallow, then passed it to the young woman next to him. She swallowed and passed it on. This was repeated until the entire group had drunk from the thermos.

Brandon then pulled a different thermos from another pile of debris and handed it to Glen. "Here," he ordered, "drink this."

Glen cautiously took the container, unscrewed the lid, and sniffed. It smelled faintly sweet, like fruit juice. "What is it?" he asked.

"We use it to help us with our transformations," Brandon said. "Drink some—it'll be fun." Then an evil smile crept onto Brandon's face. "Besides, you have no choice."

Suddenly Glen understood. Dolph had killed one of the members of their clan, and now he, Glen, was going to have to be a replacement for that lost member . . . whether he wanted to join their band or not. "But I don't know if I . . ." he began. "You see, I'm not sure if—"

"Drink!" the others shouted.

Seeing that he truly had no choice, Glen took a sip.

"Finish it," Brandon said flatly. "*Now.*"

And so, Glen drained the thermos to the last drop.

"There," he said angrily, handing the thermos back to Brandon. "Now what? Am I going to grow fangs and start—" But suddenly, the room began to spin.

"Wh—what's happening?" Glen mumbled through numb lips as he heard the others chanting in a strange language. To his horror, he saw their bodies melt. They seemed to flow into different shapes, just as his own body was rearranging itself under his skin. Then, all at once, Glen found himself looking at a group of wolves sitting in a circle around him, panting hungrily as saliva trailed from their open jaws.

Am I a wolf, too? he asked himself, quickly looking down at his body. And then he realized that he had made the worst mistake of his life. "You—you don't want me to join you, do you?" Glen whispered to the wolves surrounding him.

"Sure we do," answered one wolf in Brandon's voice. "We want you to join us for dinner. Only—"

"*I'm* the dinner," Glen finished the sentence for him, his soft white fur trembling, awaiting his fate as a defenseless white rabbit trapped by a circle of hungry wolves.

THE END

Bloody Laundry

⊱—:—⟨•⟩—•⊙•—⟨•⟩—:—⊰

THE MORNING SKY WAS DARK WITH THE PROMISE of a coming storm. Ellen couldn't stop shivering as she waited for her friends, Cybil and Nola. The three of them always walked to school together, but this morning Ellen wished she'd gotten a ride from her mom instead. It looked like they were going to get drenched. Finally she saw the two girls approaching from farther down the street.

"Come on, you guys," she shouted as she took a few steps toward them. "I'm freezing to death!"

"Don't be such a wimp!" Cybil called back. "This is spring weather where I come from in Chicago."

"They say it's going to snow later today," Nola added in her usual serious tone as they drew closer.

"Well, I don't care if it does." Ellen fell in beside her friends. "As long as I don't have to be outside in it."

As if in response to Ellen's comment, a light rain began to fall. Huddling under their umbrellas, the three girls followed their usual path through the woods.

During the summer, this was the best part of the day. Ellen loved walking through the cool shade under the trees, following the crooked stream that flowed there. But today the bare branches looked like dead claws, and everything was eerily silent, except for the faint dripping of rainwater off the tree limbs. Although nobody said anything, all three girls felt the strange silence and walked a little faster than they normally did. Then they all stopped dead in their tracks when they saw a figure bending over the edge of the stream ahead of them.

"Who's that?" asked Cybil, pointing at the crouching figure. "I've never seen her before."

Ellen peered through the misty gloom at the old woman. It looked like she was bending over something in the water. "What is she doing out here on a horrible day like this?" Ellen wondered out loud.

"Weird," muttered Nola. "Let's go around her."

Ellen nodded her agreement. Something about the whole situation was odd, and she suddenly felt nervous.

As the three girls began to edge off the path, Ellen, who didn't want to startle the woman, called out "Hello" to her as they came closer.

She didn't answer, but Ellen was now close enough to see the woman's greasy black hair and the faded, shapeless dress she was wearing. Unbelievably it looked like the woman was doing her laundry in the stream. Ellen was about to make a comment to her friends when she saw what the woman was washing and her words caught in her throat. She was washing clothes so stained with blood that the part of the stream where she knelt was a pool of red. There was blood streaked on the woman's arms up to her elbows, and tiny fingers of red slipped into the current, washing downstream.

Ellen stopped abruptly and heard Cybil and Nola stumbling to a halt behind her. She heard one of them gasp as they also got a glimpse of the horrible sight.

"Do you think she killed somebody?" demanded Nola in a shrill voice, backing away. Although Nola had spoken loudly, the woman gave no sign that she even noticed the three girls.

"I don't know," whispered Ellen.

"Well, let's not stick around to find out," insisted Cybil. "Let's get out of here!"

The girls broke into a run. Stumbling over roots, dodging tree branches and prickly bushes, the three friends fled in the direction of their school. Every few feet, one of them would cast a panicked glance over her shoulder to see if the horrible laundress was chasing after them, but she seemed to have vanished in the mist.

Ellen broke out of the trees first, with Nola and Cybil close behind, then together they raced across the meadow to the safety of the school football field. Erin Smith, the teenage daughter of the PE teacher, was jogging around the dirt track that circled the field. Ellen called out as they ran toward the older girl.

"What is it?" Erin asked in alarm when she saw their panicked faces. "What's the matter?"

"We saw . . ." Ellen gasped, "we saw something horrible back along the stream."

"It was an old woman," added Nola in a breathy voice. "And she—"

"She was washing clothes covered with blood!" Cybil finished.

Erin's eyes widened in disbelief. "What?" she asked. "What exactly did you see?"

Ellen had recovered her breath by this point and attempted to tell their story as calmly as she could. When she finished, she shuddered with the awful memory.

"And the old woman never said a word," Nola added. "She never even looked up."

Erin considered what she'd just heard. Then she looked at the three girls with confidence. "I know what you saw," she said. "You've just described a *Bean-nighe*."

"Ben Neeyeh?" asked Cybil, puzzled by the strange word.

Erin nodded. "Yeah, I've heard about them from my grandmother. They're supposed to be the ghosts of women who died in childbirth. They're fated to wash their bloody laundry until the day when they normally would have died."

The three friends looked at one another in disbelief. "But what does it mean?" Ellen asked. "Why would we see her there all of a sudden? We walk the same way to school every day and have never seen her before."

Erin glanced over their heads toward the forest. Then she leaned forward and whispered slowly, "The *Bean-nighe* is only seen by those who are about to die."

"What?!" Ellen yelped, backing up a step.

Cybil put her hands on her hips. "Yeah, right!" she scoffed.

Erin straightened. "You're the ones who brought her up, not me."

"But," Nola protested, "we *all* saw her. What does that mean?"

"I don't know," answered Erin with a shrug. "Maybe it only counts for the one who saw her first."

In spite of her skepticism about Erin's story, Ellen felt an icy layer forming around her heart. "But-but who was that?" she stammered.

"Oh, come on!" Cybil exclaimed angrily. "This is crazy. It was probably some old beggar woman." She looked up at the sky, now almost black. "We're about to get soaked, and first period is starting. I'm outta here." And with that she stormed off toward the school.

Deciding that she was probably right, Nola and Ellen said good-bye to Erin and followed their friend to class.

"Erin's just trying to scare us," Nola whispered.

"Yeah," Ellen whispered back, hoping that Nola was right.

The rain grew stronger throughout the day, and lightning filled the sky. By the end of the afternoon, icy hail was coming down in sheets. Rather than walk home in the downpour, Ellen called her mom at work to see if she could drive her and Nola home. Cybil, who truly loved the cold weather, decided she'd rather walk.

"Watch out for the bloody laundry lady," Ellen joked. During the day, they had come to agree with Cybil that all they had seen was a beggar woman washing her clothes. Now they were practically convinced that what they thought was blood was only some kind of wine or food stain.

"In this weather?" Cybil asked with raised eyebrows. "No laundry is *that* important!" She burst out laughing and headed for the forest.

※ ※ ※

By the time Ellen sat down to dinner, the hail had turned to snow. "Looks like we're in for a real blizzard," her dad said as he came to the table after watching the news.

"Really?" Ellen asked, a faint stir of excitement running through her at the thought of school being canceled. "I sure hope—"

But the ring of the telephone interrupted her, and she excused herself to answer it. It was Cybil's mother, asking if she'd seen Cybil. "She never came home from school," the worried woman said. "Please, Ellen, can you tell me where she is?"

But all Ellen could offer was the news that Cybil had decided to walk home after school by herself.

Over the next few hours, as the wind rose and the snow began to fall more heavily, policemen searched the neighborhood for Cybil. Her body was found within a few hours, lying halfway in the stream in the woods.

"They say she probably slipped and fell," Ellen explained in a tense telephone conversation with Nola after the initial shock had worn off. "She must have hit her head on a rock or something, and froze to death before she came to."

"Do you really believe that?" Nola asked.

"What do you mean?" Ellen returned almost defensively. "Of course I do. Don't you?"

"It just seems so . . . sudden," Nola answered. "I—I don't know what to believe."

They were both silent for a moment, thinking of their friend. Then Nola asked hesitantly, "What about the woman we saw this morning?"

"What about her?" Ellen demanded harshly. She wasn't about to admit that the same thought had already crept into her head. She had been relieved that if Erin *had* been telling the truth, then at least they now knew who had seen the washing woman first. Sure it had made Ellen feel disgusted with herself for thinking such a horrible thing, but she had to admit she was glad *she* wasn't the one who was found dead in the stream.

"Well," Nola continued, "maybe the woman we saw really was that *Bean-nighe* thing Erin was talking about."

"And you're happy Cybil was the one to see it first?" Ellen said, accusing her friend of her own selfish thought.

Nola sounded shocked. "No! I'm wondering if Erin was right. Maybe the curse counts for *everyone* who sees the woman!"

Now Ellen felt really scared. "Look, Nola, Cybil's mom said the police told her it was an accident. That's good enough for me." She searched for an excuse to hang up. "Anyway, I've got to get off the phone now. My mom wants to use it."

"Okay," Nola said, unconvinced. "I'll see you tomorrow . . . I hope."

҈ ҈ ҈

By morning, thick drifts of snow had piled up overnight, and the radio announcer reported that her school would be closed for the day. Ellen's wish had come true, but her parents weren't so lucky. Their offices were both staying open, so Ellen asked her dad to drop her off at Nola's house on his way to work.

By unspoken agreement, neither of the girls mentioned the strange woman they had seen the previous day. Still, they couldn't help talking about Cybil and how much they missed her.

By mid-morning, the snow began falling again, and soon after, while Ellen and Nola were watching TV, the electricity went out. With a groan, Nola picked up the phone to call her parents, who had also gone to work. That was when the girls realized the phone lines were dead, too.

"Now what are we going to do?" Ellen wondered out loud, a feeling of panic slowly rising within her.

"How about making some lunch, then going out back and building a snow fort?" suggested Nola, who didn't seem to be bothered at all.

"Yeah!" exclaimed Ellen, immediately forgetting her fears. "Maybe we can get some of the other kids from the block to come over so we can have a snowball war!"

Soon they were happily hunched over peanut butter and jelly sandwiches, cracking each other up with silly stories about some of last winter's snowball fights. Ellen was in the middle of describing how she pounded one of the boys from their band class when Nola ɔegan making a strange sound.

"What?" Ellen asked, thinking the other girl was trying to say something. "I didn't understand you."

Gagging uncontrollably, Nola pushed herself away from the table. That's when Ellen realized something was terribly wrong. Her friend's face was turning a bright red, and her hands were clutching helplessly at her throat.

"Nola!" Ellen screamed. She tried pounding on her

friend's back, but Nola's horrible choking only became worse. In desperation, Ellen grabbed her friend from behind, wrapped her arms around Nola's chest like she had seen on TV, and squeezed.

But nothing happened, and Nola's face was now changing from red to blue and her lips were turning a horrible shade of purple. With her veins swelling on her forehead as if they were about to pop, Nola fell to her knees. She turned an agonized face toward Ellen, then fell to the floor in a deadly silence. Then her body relaxed, and the color completely drained from her face.

"Nola?" Ellen said in a small voice. Then she screamed, "No!" and ran out of the house.

She had no clear idea of where she was going. All she knew was that she had to get away from her friend's body, and all she heard over and over again were Erin's words: "The *Bean-nighe* is only seen by those who are about to die."

Suddenly feeling the cold air going right through her thin turtleneck, Ellen realized that she had run out of Nola's house without her jacket. Panicking, she looked around. It was hard to recognize where she was. Everything was white, and the swirling snow made it impossible for her to see more than a few feet in front of her. To make matters worse, with the electricity down there were no streetlamps or house lights to form landmarks.

"I am *not* going to die!" she said out loud to no one. "It's just a coincidence. That's all it is—a horrible coincidence."

She began walking in what she thought was the right direction toward her house, but before long she was shivering so hard her teeth were chattering. She tried to angle herself toward the sidewalk and ended up stumbling into a street sign. By squinting, she could barely make out the letters, and she happily realized that she was about five blocks away from home. *No problem*, she told herself. *I've done this walk hundreds of times before . . . but not in weather like this*. Ignoring her traitorous thoughts, Ellen struggled forward toward what she hoped was her house.

Soon her world narrowed to the patch of snow directly in front of her feet. She walked like an old woman, bent over and shaking, breaking into fits of coughing, and murmuring the word *coincidence* over and over again.

When she finally reached her own street, it felt as if a huge weight had been lifted from her. She broke into a quick shuffle as she hurried toward the warmth and safety of her home. Before she knew it, her yard was in front of her, and she ran up the front walk and flung herself through the door. It took a long time for her numbed brain to register that the house was dark. Then she remembered that the electricity was dead.

First things first, she thought as another spasm of coughing clenched her chest. She stumbled down the dark hallway to the bathroom and reached into the medicine cabinet for the cough medicine. She knew from experience that the taste was horrible, so she quickly gulped down a couple of mouthfuls.

Suddenly pain shot through her with such intensity that it pitched her to the floor. Her throat began to burn, and her stomach felt like it was being torn apart. She tried to scream, but the walls of her throat had swollen shut. Her weakened body flopped on the floor like a fish out of water, and her vision dimmed. Whatever she had swallowed, it wasn't cough medicine.

Then, like a hideous joke, the lights flickered back on—just in time for Ellen to see that she had drunk from a bottle of her mother's hair dye. *Coincidence—yeah, right!* was her final, mocking thought before the poisonous liquid took her.

THE END

The Good Deed

CORY WANDERED DOWN TO THE EDGE OF THE lake to stare at the water. Behind him, he could hear his two sisters shouting as they chased each other around the campsite. Across the lake, he could see his dad wading thigh-deep in the cold lake water, casting his fishing line out onto the still surface. His mom was reading under the shade of a tree, not too far from where his father was catching dinner.

Cory sighed and flopped down on the coarse grass that fringed the shores of the lake. He had always enjoyed coming on these camping trips with his family. But this time something felt different. He felt, well, kind of bored. After all, why should he be hanging around with his family? He was going into junior high in September. None of the other guys would be caught dead taking a trip with their families anymore.

"Yep," Cory said out loud to no one, "I'm getting too old for this kind of thing."

Realizing that there was nothing he could do about it now, he got to his feet and set off on a tour of the lake.

Maybe he'd find something interesting. He caught his dad's attention and waved his arm in a circle, indicating the path around the lake. His dad nodded and waved back. *Good,* Cory thought. *At least he's not going to make me fish with him.*

This was the first time the family had been to this lake, so Cory took his time on the trail that wove along the shore. Fed by a number of small streams from the melting snow on the mountains that surrounded it, the lake lay in a bowl at the base of the towering peaks. At various points, clumps of pine trees grew right to the water's edge, and Cory had to kick his way through a thick carpet of pine needles. Sometimes the trail would disappear altogether, hidden by boulders that had tumbled down from the eroded peaks.

Cory tried hard to remain bored with everything, but he had to admit it was kind of fun, scrambling over the warm rocks, trying to sneak up on lizards basking in the sun.

At one point Cory climbed over a large pile of boulders and found himself on the arm of a small, sheltered bay. The water was as still as glass there, and he stared at the reflection of sky and mountains that came off of it. Then he picked up a rock and, with one swift throw, instantly shattered the image. *Maybe it'll scare the fish toward Dad,* he thought as he descended into the tiny cove and made his way around it.

On the opposite side of the lake, Cory found a faint trail leading away from the water. It appeared to follow a narrow brook. "Maybe it's some kind of game trail," he muttered to himself. Curious, he decided to follow it.

The trail ran deep into the woods, hugging the brook's edge, but after a while it veered away from the water and zigzagged toward a clearing. On one side of the clearing was a cabin built of dark brown wood that rested on a base of large, gray rocks. Cory didn't see anyone around and, glancing at his watch, decided there wasn't enough time to check it out. *Besides*, he reasoned, *it's probably private property, anyway*. Quietly ducking back into the trees, he returned to the lakeside to finish his tour and get back to camp in time for dinner. Maybe he'd come back to explore the cabin before the end of the trip.

兴 兴 兴

"Going to do some fishing today?" his dad asked him the next morning after breakfast.

Cory shrugged. He hadn't really thought about it, but it seemed like a better choice than doing nothing. "Yeah, sure," he answered.

Cory fetched his rod and tackle so his dad could get the line ready with its red-and-white bobber and tiny golden hook. Then the two of them wandered down to the lake.

Nearly three hours later, Cory figured the fish must be laughing their gills off. Cory's dad had caught only one fish and Cory hadn't caught any. Discouraged, they returned to camp for lunch.

"Good thing we're not living off what Cory catches," his sister Kirsti teased.

"Yeah," his other sister, Nicole, agreed. "We'd starve to death."

Cory made a face at them and took another bite of his sandwich. He thought about the private bay he had found yesterday. *There've got to be fish in there*, he thought. "Oh yeah?" he said to his sisters. "Well, I bet I catch some fish this afternoon."

"What kind—goldfish?" Kirsti asked sarcastically.

Nicole thought this was the funniest thing she'd heard during the whole trip and howled with laughter. Cory ignored the brats. "There's a place I want to try on the other side of the lake," he said to his dad. "I'll catch up with you later, okay?"

"Okay, but don't wander off too far and get lost," his dad warned. "It can get tricky out here, and you could easily lose your way."

Cory nodded in agreement, wolfed down the rest of his lunch, and grabbed his fishing rod. Soon he was back at what he was beginning to think of as "his" cove. He climbed down the rocks to the water's edge and found a comfortable shelf of rock to sit on. He baited his hook and cast his line far out into the middle of the water. Then, letting the line rest on his finger so he could feel the tug of a hungry fish, Cory closed his eyes and relaxed.

Suddenly he heard a huge splash, and his eyes flew open. *I must have fallen asleep*, he thought. Looking at the horizon he was surprised to see that the sun had already sunk so low it was touching the tops of the peaks to the west. He sat up and looked toward the water to see what had awakened him, and saw a small, inflatable raft floating toward shore. It was being pushed along on the waves created by someone frantically thrashing in the center of the bay. Seeing that it was a girl, Cory first thought it was one of his sisters.

But we don't have a boat like that, he quickly told himself. *And Kirsti and Nicole know how to swim. That girl looks like she's drowning!* Without another thought, Cory kicked off his tennis shoes and dove off the rocks into the water.

The cold hit him like a blow to the chest, and he came up gasping. Then, with a burst of energy, he knifed through the water toward the yellow rubber boat. He grabbed it by a rope that hung from its side and pulled it toward the frantic girl.

"Hang on!" he yelled. "I'm coming!"

She didn't seem to hear him over the sound of her own choking breath and kept flailing her arms in the air. Finally Cory reached her and grabbed one of her arms. Feeling another person nearby, the girl clenched her arm around Cory's neck in a death hold.

His breath practically choked off, Cory began to panic as the girl refused to loosen her grip. With no other choice, he punched the girl hard on her shoulder until he managed to jog her loose.

"Are you trying to kill me, too?" Cory gasped, reaching for the dinghy and pulling it toward them. "Here's the boat. Grab it!"

Her eyes wide, the terrified girl swung her arm over the edge of the boat and held on with a white-knuckled grip.

"All right," Cory said, breathing heavily while he helped keep the girl's head above water. "Can you climb into the boat?"

The girl nodded. Then, with Cory's help, she slid over the side and into the small dinghy, followed by her exhausted savior.

For what seemed like ages, the two lay in the bottom of the boat, silently gasping. Finally Cory sat up. "Can you help me paddle this thing to shore?" he asked.

The girl took a few more breaths, then nodded. "I think so," she said.

Cory glanced around. "Looks like the oars are gone." He shrugged. "Oh, well. Let's get going."

They each took one side of the boat and paddled with their hands until the dinghy slowly slid across the cove to the small trail Cory had seen yesterday. When the boat's tip finally bounced against the shore, Cory thought it was the finest sound he'd ever heard. He quickly clambered out of the boat, and the girl followed him.

"Thank you," she said shyly. "You saved my life." She held out her hand. "My name's Sadie."

Cory shook her hand and introduced himself. "Well, I'm just glad you're all right," he said, a little embarrassed. "But tell me—how did you fall in? It's not exactly wavy out there."

Sadie looked up the trail in the direction of the cabin. "I'm here staying with my grandfather. While he was gone today, I decided to take the boat out. I'm not supposed to," she added, biting her lip. "You see, I can't swim. For some reason, my grandfather won't teach me."

Cory shivered in the cool air of the late afternoon. The sun had now fallen behind the mountains, and the bay was completely in shadow. The girl still hadn't answered his question, so he asked again. "But I still don't understand why you fell in."

"I'm not sure, either," the girl said, shrugging. "I was bending over to look at something on the bottom of the lake, and I guess I lost my balance." She stopped for a moment and noticed Cory shivering. "Do you want to come up to the cabin? My grandfather should be back by now, and you could get warm by the fire."

Cory thought about his family around their own fire and hesitated for a moment, knowing he should get back. Then he figured, *Why not? They'll understand. After all, I'm a hero now.* "Okay," he told Sadie. "I am kind of cold."

When they got to the cabin, Sadie's grandfather was indeed home, and he jumped up from the table when the two soaking kids came through the door.

"Sadie!" he exclaimed. "What happened to you?" He looked at Cory suspiciously.

Sadie threw herself into her grandfather's arms. "Grandpa," she said, her face buried in his sweater, "I'm sorry!"

The old man held her closely while Cory squirmed uncomfortably under the old man's sharp blue eyes.

"For what, honey?" the old man asked, his eyes still fixed on Cory.

"I know I'm not supposed to, but I took the boat out and it tipped over." She looked at Cory and pointed. "He saved me, Grandpa."

"What?" the old man demanded, holding Sadie at arm's length and looking sternly at her. "You took the boat in the water?"

Sadie nodded tearfully. "I'm sorry, Grandpa. I'll never do it again."

"And you fell in," he said in the same tone. "You see how dangerous it is?"

"Yes," Sadie sniffed. "I would have drowned if it hadn't been for Cory."

Cory had been watching the old man's face as it showed first surprise, then relief. Now he saw something that looked like fear.

Turning abruptly away from Sadie, her grandfather strode over to the window and looked outside. Night had come quickly after the sun had disappeared behind the mountains, and the clearing around the cabin was now almost fully dark. Muttering under his breath, the old man began pacing from window to window, yanking them open in order to pull the shutters closed.

"Bolt the door," he ordered Sadie.

Seemingly as mystified as Cory by all this sudden activity, Sadie automatically obeyed.

"Excuse me, sir," Cory began, "but what's going on?"

"You foolish boy!" the old man said angrily. "That was a nixie you snatched her from." He finished closing the last shutter and turned to face Cory angrily.

"The what?" asked Cory, completely confused and a little frightened by the old man's behavior.

"A *nixie*," Sadie's grandfather repeated, as if that said it all. He made a visible effort to control himself, then explained further.

"Nixies are ancient beings—as old as the hills, as old as the trees. They live in lakes, ponds—in *all* bodies of water." The old man's voice dropped lower. "Nobody knows what they look like, because they can change into anything they want. But no matter what shape they choose, they hate humans—and will often try to kill them."

Cory didn't know whether to laugh at this wild talk or run in fear of the crazy old man. He looked helplessly at Sadie, who was standing beside the door and watching the whole scene very quietly. Something about her lack of reaction made Cory more nervous than anything else.

"Where I come from," the old man continued in a husky voice, "it is said to be bad luck to save a drowning person. Fate has offered that person to the nixie, who must have at least one human sacrifice per year."

"But that's crazy!" cried Cory. "You can't just stand by and let someone drown. Besides, if it hadn't been for me, your granddaughter would be dead."

The old man brought his hands up to his face. "I know," he said, his voice muffled and strained with emotion. "And for saving her, I'm grateful."

Cory was afraid the old guy was going to burst into tears. He turned toward Sadie. "Listen," he said, "it's really late, and my folks are probably getting worried. I think I'd better go."

"I don't think that's a good idea," she said quietly.

Halfway to the door, Cory stopped. A terrible thought rose up from the depths of his mind and seized hold of his brain with claws of sheer horror.

The old man said the nixie could look like anything it wants, his mind raced. *What if the real Sadie was already dead by the time I woke up to save her?*

Sadie saw the expression on Cory's face and blanched. "What—what are you thinking?" she asked, sounding a bit defensive. "I just don't think you should be wandering around out there after dark. If my grandfather is right, this nixie thing might get you."

Cory felt his mouth grow dry as he tried to answer. *That makes sense,* he thought, trying to stay calm. *No, it doesn't,* he scolded himself. *Her grandfather is just trying to scare us with that crazy story. Well, she may have fallen for it, but*

I'm out of here. "Uh, my family," Cory said weakly. "I've got to get back to my mom, dad, and sisters."

Sadie opened her mouth to answer when something thudded—or did it splash?—against the door of the small cabin. With a scream, she jumped away. "Look!" she whispered. She held one hand over her mouth and pointed with the other at the bottom of the door.

There was another splashy thud, harder than before, and the wood of the door frame creaked in response. Cory slowly turned to see what Sadie was pointing at and saw a growing stain of water spread through the crack under the door . . . as if something very big and wet were standing on the other side.

Feeling his control begin to slip, Cory unglued his eyes from the horrible stain and stared at the old man, then at Sadie. They were both trembling, and in a flash of terror Cory knew he had made a mistake. Sadie wasn't the nixie, after all, and if her grandfather was right, the *real* nixie was behind that door!

Another wet thud threatened to break down the thin barrier between Cory and the wet being that was outside, a wet being that was probably a nixie who was very angry with *him*.

THE END

39

SOS

>━━┥━◆>━•━⊖━•━<◆>━┥━≼

GINA'S FATHER POINTED TO A YACHT NESTLED IN a slip at the end of the dock. "That's the one," he said. "Home sweet home for the next four weeks."

Gina let go of her mom's hand and ran down the length of the wooden dock for her first look at the boat her father had rented for their vacation. He had just finished some big project that had kept him so occupied for the last seven months that Gina's mom had begun making jokes about being a single mother. Finally he had finished, and to celebrate, he had rented this yacht from one of his clients.

Carefully Gina inspected the outside of the boat. If she was going to spend four weeks on this thing, she wanted to be sure there were no cracks or holes in it.

The yacht was just over forty feet long and had two masts—one in the front and one at the back. It was painted a blinding white, and it had polished wooden handrails along both sides of its deck. Along the back, Gina read the boat's name, *Penny Dreadful*.

"Well?" asked her mother as they caught up to her. "Is everything all right?"

"What does *Penny Dreadful* mean?" Gina asked, pointing to the name written on the back of the boat.

Her father laughed. "The woman who owns this yacht writes books. *Penny dreadful* is what they used to call a cheap, action-packed paperback."

"Odd name for a boat," Gina commented. "Well, it looks okay from the outside. What's it like inside?"

"There's only one way to find out," her dad said, pointing to the doorway that led into the cabin.

Inside was much nicer than Gina had expected it to be. There was a large area that was a combination living room and kitchen. It was filled with every appliance she could think of, and all of them gleamed like new. The kitchen counters, made of rich, dark wood, were spotless as well, and the carpeting in the cabin was soft and clean. Continuing forward, Gina found two bedrooms—the first, a larger room with a double bed, and beyond that a small one up in the front of the hull. All of the furniture was modern, and the beds seemed comfortable. Gina nodded approvingly and went topside to give her dad her okay. Then she helped her parents unload the food and supplies they had packed for the trip.

Finally it was time to shove off, and Gina could hardly contain her excitement as her father untied the ropes that held them to the dock. Then, with one strong push from her father, the sailboat floated out into the calm waters of the marina. With Gina and her parents shouting orders and pretending they were pirates setting out to loot and plunder, the three glided smoothly out to sea.

Gina quickly grew accustomed to life on a boat. She had been afraid she would be seasick, but to her delight she found that the constant motion didn't bother her at all. When she mentioned this to her father, he laughed and pointed out that they were in pretty calm waters. Still, Gina felt that she could withstand whatever the ocean was going to throw at her.

Her parents' plan was to leisurely sail among the islands that dotted the waters in this part of the world. They had no specific goal in mind and were free to stay as long as they wanted on any particular island.

The first landing they made was on a small mountain poking up above the blue water. It was covered with lush tropical growth that looked like green velvet from a distance. As they drew closer, however, Gina could see long curves of shining white sand just waiting for her to lay a towel on. After her father had dropped anchor in a small bay, he rowed Gina and her mother to shore where they all sunbathed for a few hours.

But as it turned out, the island was deserted, and the family got bored. They decided to spend only a day there, lazing in the sun and exploring the dense jungle.

For Gina, the vacation became a series of minor variations on that first island stopover, except some of the islands had people living on them. If it wasn't for a friendly old man on another yacht docked next to them on one of the populated islands, Gina would have really gotten tired of the same old routine. But the old man was fascinating and full of real-life pirate tales that held her captivated for hours.

The man's name was Craig, and Gina's dad had moored next to his boat in the tiny marina that served the local islanders. With his brown, leathery skin marked with millions of tiny wrinkles, Craig, Gina thought, looked as if he'd spent his entire life baking under the sun.

He confirmed Gina's suspicions when he answered a question her father had asked. "Ayup, I've been sailing these waters for well on forty-five years, now."

"Forty-five years," Gina repeated in wonder. "Wow! You must have seen every inch of every island . . . everywhere."

Craig shrugged. "Seen a lot of 'em, I guess."

"We're on a casual tour," said Gina's father. "Any advice you can give us?"

The old sailor thought for a moment, then nodded. "Ayup. Things are a little rough yonder round Leeward Isles. There's been a gang of pirates that's been causing a lot of trouble out there."

"Pirates?" Gina's mom asked doubtfully. "In this day and age?"

"Aye," Craig answered firmly. "Some things never change, except the boats they sail and the weapons they use."

"Is it dangerous?" asked Gina's dad.

"Can be. But if you stay well away from the Leewards, you shouldn't have any problem. You have maps, right?"

When Gina's dad answered that they did, Craig clambered over and offered to point out the areas he'd been talking about. He disappeared below deck with Gina's dad, and the two men were gone for over an hour.

"I sure hope Craig will show my dad some exciting places to explore," Gina mumbled under her breath. "I'm tired of wandering around from island to island and sunbathing all day."

Gina and her parents spent two days on the small island, poking around the shops and taking bike rides through the interior. Gina was glad they weren't leaving right away. She was fascinated by their neighbor, Craig, and spent a lot of time listening to his incredible collection of stories. Pirates, old and new; fantastic creatures; glorious sea battles; mysterious ghost ships—the old man never seemed to run out of tales to tell.

Gina's favorite was the legend of the lost ship *Azrael*. According to Craig, the *Azrael* was the ghost of an old slave ship that had been carrying a full cargo of children when a fierce storm blew in. The captain, greedy to get his cargo of children to port so he could sell them, tried to sail through the storm even as it grew into a tremendous hurricane. The ship sank with all hands on deck, drowning the children who were still chained below.

"And ever since then," Craig said in a low voice, "the *Azrael* has sailed these waters, trying to make it to port. And the captain, even greedier in death, is said to be still searching for more children to add to his grisly cargo."

Gina shuddered in appreciation. Then, when Craig returned to his chores, she scampered off to write down as much of the story as she could remember. She wanted to tell it to her friends back home.

When they left the island, Gina's dad made sure to steer them away from the Leeward Isles. Instead, he pointed the *Penny Dreadful* toward a distant cluster of dots on the map, labeled the Hundred Atolls.

"I'm relatively sure we won't run into pirates there," he said, adding with a grin, "*if* there really are any."

But when they were a little less than two days away from the Hundred Atolls, something odd began to happen. They noticed a small speck—probably a boat—on the horizon behind them . . . and it appeared to be following them.

"Maybe it's one of the other boats we met?" Gina wondered out loud when she pointed out the distant vessel.

"We'll know for sure in a couple of days," her father said. "The Atolls are the only islands in this direction. We'll probably see them there."

But by the end of that day, Gina wasn't sure what the other ship was up to. As the setting sun turned the sky and sea into competing shades of gold, it was plain that the other ship had drawn closer as if it was, well, *chasing* after them. Now, instead of a formless black speck, Gina could just make out the billowing white sails of a very large ship.

Gina saw her parents having an animated discussion, but when they saw that she was watching they ducked below into the galley. Not wasting another moment, Gina crept closer to hear what they were talking about.

"I know," her father was saying, "but the simple fact that they're gaining on us means they must be moving under power."

"But that could be for any number of reasons," her mother answered. "It doesn't mean they're pirates."

"True. But after all those stories Craig was telling us, I'm just a little suspicious of any boat that has its sails up *and* its motor running. Especially when it's coming our way!"

Gina held her breath and strained to hear. *Pirates!* she thought, feeling electric tingles that were part fear, part excitement running through her.

"Look," her father continued, "all I'm saying is that it doesn't hurt us to lose a night's sleep. We'll put up full sail and keep an eye on the ship. That should put us comfortably ahead of it. Or, at the very least, keep us even."

"All right," her mother agreed. "That makes sense." Then she gave a small chuckle. "Looks like we won't be saving that coffee for the return trip."

True to her father's plan, they put up all the sails they had, causing the yacht to fairly leap across the tops of the waves. Gina kept her parents company as long as she could, but eventually made her way to her bunk. She had tried to ask them a few questions about what was going on, but had only gotten clipped, vague answers. *Anyway*, she thought as she dozed off, *at least down below I don't have to look at their tense faces.*

⫛ ⫛ ⫛

The next morning Gina was up with the sun, and an ominous sight greeted her when she went on deck. Her mom and dad were sitting at the tiller, sipping mugs of coffee. They both looked more grim than they had the night before, and Gina could easily see why.

The ship behind them had drawn even closer in the night. Now it was easy to see that it was a gigantic sailing ship, much larger than the tiny yacht she was on. Its enormous sails were pulling away from its masts, and looked like thick, billowing clouds hovering over the water. Gina, unable to see the bright gleam of paint in the sunlight, wondered if the ship behind them was hidden in the shadow of its sails or if it was painted some dark color.

47

"Is it really pirates?" Gina asked her parents after staring at the pursuing ship.

"I don't know," her father answered. "Whoever they are, they're in quite a hurry."

"Maybe we should start our engine," Gina's mother suggested quietly.

With one last glance at the pursuing ship, Gina's father nodded and went below, and after a few moments the powerful engines coughed into life with a reassuring rumble that gently vibrated the wooden deck. Instantly their yacht surged forward and began pulling away from the mysterious ship that trailed them.

The morning passed in tense silence. It seemed to Gina that the ship behind them had taken over her parents' thoughts. They absently replied to anything she said, and their eyes kept returning to the black ship behind them. It was her parents' obvious worry that frightened Gina the most, and her mind conjured up terrifying pictures of horrible men swarming over the yacht and murdering her parents right in front of her eyes.

But even going as fast as they could, as the day lengthened, the distance between the two ships grew shorter.

"How can they be moving so fast?" Gina's father snapped to no one in particular. Muttering curses, he stomped down below to try and squeeze more power out of their own tiny engine. Gina's mother, looking extremely tense, went down with him, and Gina could hear the two of them whispering in frightened voices.

The ship was close enough now for Gina to see that it was a huge wooden vessel—at least three times the length of their yacht—with five separate sails that she could see. The middle part of the ship was lower than its front and back, and the whole craft was built of dark wood.

As Gina looked at the huge billowing sails, something about them seemed strange to her, but she couldn't figure out what. She then turned her eyes to the deck, where she could barely make out figures moving slowly about. That meant that they probably could see Gina and her parents, but for some reason they made no sign of greeting or of recognition. Gina shivered slightly. Obviously the people who were on board were not friendly fellow-travelers.

It was Gina's father who later pointed out the problem that had subconsciously bothered her. "Those sails sure are odd," he mumbled, staring at the pursuing ship. Then suddenly he opened his eyes wide in surprise and pointed at the dark vessel. "That's impossible!" he gasped.

"What?" Gina asked, peering at the black ship.

"The sails . . ." He groped for words. "The sails . . . they're pointing the wrong way!"

Suddenly Gina understood. She looked up at the sails of their own boat. The wind was pushing from the left, blowing the sails out and over the other side of the boat. But the sails of the black ship stood straight out from the masts, as if the wind was coming from directly behind.

Even Gina, with her short experience sailing, knew this was impossible. And her heart seemed to freeze to a halt as a horrible thought exploded in her mind. *The Azrael*, she thought in terror. *It's coming for me!*

She turned to her father, fear stretching her face into a mask of wide eyes and a gaping mouth. "We've got to go faster, Dad," she urged. "Craig told me about that ship—it's a ghost ship looking for children to sell as slaves!"

Gina's father looked at her strangely, and she could tell he thought she was so scared she was talking crazy. He rested a hand on her head. "We'll be okay," he promised. "We should have the first of the Atolls in sight by late this afternoon, and I don't think whoever's on that ship will try anything when we're that close to land."

"Please go faster," Gina urged.

Seeing his daughter's tremendous fear, her father nodded and went back below to talk things over with her mother.

Gina glanced back at the horrible ship. She watched in amazement and terror as the terrible black ship drew closer. It was as if her thoughts had given it renewed power!

Now, the sails looked tattered and leprous and seemed to glow with pale bolts of lightning that flickered around the masts. The dark wood of the hull revealed itself to be black with slime, like something from the bottom of the sea. And the huge bow made no wave as it pushed closer. It was as if the ancient wood offered no resistance to the blue-green water—as if it didn't sail on the sea, but floated above it.

Gina heard a gasp of sharply drawn breath at her side and turned to see her mother standing with one hand to her mouth. "Mom," Gina sobbed, pointing to the ghost ship, "we've got to get out of here! Can't we go any faster?"

Without answering, her mother turned and went back down to the engines.

Gina remained at the rail, hypnotized by the thing that was chasing them. In horror, she watched the figures of the crew, staring at their ragged clothing, torn so badly that it showed glimpses of their skin, pale as a fish belly. And all of the disgusting figures had a terribly bloated, diseased appearance, too, as they snapped to the attention of a grinning skeleton that stood at the highest deck of the ship, with its bony arms folded across its chest.

But even worse was the huddled group of children standing at the front of the ship. Although dressed in many different styles of clothing, they all had in common a heavy iron chain running from one neck collar to the next, connecting them in a long line.

"No," Gina mumbled. "Not me. I'm not going to be one of them."

Suddenly an explosion slammed her to the deck. Black smoke poured out of the open hatch that led below deck.

"They're attacking!" Gina screamed as the yacht lurched to one side, then began tilting slowly backward.

She fought her way up the slanting deck to peer through the oily smoke into the salon where her parents had been. Water was bubbling up from below, and the room was already filling with water. Horrified, Gina saw her mother floating facedown in the dirty seawater. "Mom!" she screamed, then looked frantically for her father, who was nowhere to be seen.

"No!" Gina screamed, throwing herself into the water to her mother's side. She rolled the body over and saw clearly that her mother was no longer alive. Then, bursting into tears, Gina starting yelling for her father like a madwoman.

Suddenly the yacht lurched, throwing the dead body of her father overboard. Gina screamed as the boat settled farther into the water. Now the saltwater was beginning to wash over the deck railings, and Gina saw faint streams begin to trickle down the steps from above. Choking on her tears, she waded to the steps and climbed onto the deck. Then, looking back for just a second, she flung herself into the water as the yacht, along with the bodies of her parents, sank.

As she paddled around in circles, crying and trying to keep her head above water, Gina suddenly felt an icy breeze wash over her wet back. Looking up through bleary eyes, she saw the black, slime-coated hull of the *Azrael* beside her. Two animate corpses were hanging from some ropes, and their decaying arms were stretched toward her. Far above them were dozens of children, their dead eyes staring down at Gina.

"No!" she screamed, then burst into furious kicking. But as hard as she tried, Gina couldn't seem to move her body. And soon, cold hands grasped her arms and began hauling her up.

"Please!" Gina pleaded as she tried to struggle. "Don't take me with you!"

But then, one of the children turned her empty eye sockets on Gina and pointed at something below her in the water. Retching with fear, Gina turned to see the body of a small girl—*her* body—sinking slowly beneath the waves.

THE END

One Hot Night

>─┼─◆>─⊙─<◆─┼─◄

ALL FIFTEEN MEMBERS OF SCOUT TROOP 391 BURST
into the clearing like an attacking army. Mr. Stone, the troop
leader, yelled orders from the rear, but the boys were too
excited at finally having reached their campsite to pay him
any attention. Shouting dares, yelling jokes, or simply
cheering, the boys dropped their packs wherever they stood
and raced around wildly.

The campsite was a large field with long, green grass.
It lay in the heart of a chain of rolling hills covered with the
light dew of early spring and dotted everywhere with
enormous oak trees. One huge tree stood in the center of the
camp. It seemed big enough to shade all of the boys under
its branches, and it stood out in the otherwise empty field
like a monument.

"Come on!" Lee shouted to his friends Steve and Roger.
"There's supposed to be a stream somewhere around here."

The three of them raced across the meadow and
plunged under the canopy of trees at the far end. Most of
the other boys were doing the same thing, and when the
stream was located, another cheer went up. Then, one by

one, the boys stripped off their sweaty shirts and dusty pants and plunged into the cool water.

Mr. Stone gave up trying to corral the troop and settled down in the middle of the now-empty field to wait. Eventually, when the soaked boys began to straggle back from the stream, he had them pitch their tents and unpack, sending a few of them back upstream to fill water jugs.

Soon it was time to prepare their meals, and a smaller, more controlled riot broke out as everyone tried to see what the others had brought to eat. There wasn't much difference in the choices—it was all freeze-dried food that could be cooked over a camp stove—but there was still a lot of heavy trading going on.

Mr. Stone had warned the boys before the trip began that he was not going to allow any fires. Even though it was only the first of May, the troop leader felt the brush was already too dry to risk having an open flame.

"I can't believe it," Lee complained to Steve and Roger as they fired up their tiny stoves. "No campfire. What kind of a camping trip is this?"

Both Steve and Roger were getting sick and tired of listening to Lee complain about not having a campfire. He hadn't let up about it since Mr. Stone had mentioned it. In fact, Lee seemed to take it personally that there were no fires allowed on the trip.

"Look at it this way," Roger suggested patiently. "At least you don't have to gather firewood."

"But no sausages, no marshmallows, no nothing," Lee muttered.

Steve made a face behind Lee's back and Roger cracked up.

"What?" Lee asked angrily as he shot them both a disgusted look. Then, seeing their innocent shrugs, he turned his attention to preparing his dinner of freeze-dried stew.

None of the dinners took long to prepare, or to eat, and soon the boys found themselves sitting around a lantern Mr. Stone had brought. For a while, they all swapped scary stories and silly jokes, but when Mr. Stone saw a storm brewing off in the distance, he sent everyone off to get ready for bed.

After their bedtime chores were finished, Lee, Roger, and Steve piled into the tent they were sharing. Lee griped a little more about the "weirdness" of sitting around a lantern instead of a fire, and that forced his two friends to tickle him until he promised to shut up. Then, listening to the grumbling sounds of thunder in the distance—which added the perfect touch to a night in the woods—the boys fell fast asleep.

The next morning the troop awoke to a drenched campsite, but the skies were clear. It would have been a beautiful beginning to a day if Lee hadn't started right out complaining again. Finally Roger and Steve had enough and left their friend alone with his grousing. Lee, feeling more sour than ever, took off by himself in the opposite direction.

Kicking his way across a meadow that looked plenty green enough to him to be a low-risk fire area, Lee muttered to himself as he stomped along. "Stone's a jerk," he grumbled. "We'd have to hold a blowtorch to this grass to catch it on fire." Plunging on with his head down, he didn't see the two kids sitting quietly in the grass in front of him and almost stumbled right over them.

They were a boy and a girl, and they seemed to be about the same age as Lee. *Probably brother and sister, if not twins,* Lee thought, noticing how much the two kids looked alike.

"Hey!" he said, surprised. "Where did you guys come from?"

"Over there," the boy answered, pointing his chin at a not-too-distant hill. "We're here with our mom and dad." He paused for a moment. "Who are you?"

"My name's Lee. I'm here with my Scout troop."

"I'm Sandy," the girl offered.

"Dan," the boy said.

Lee looked curiously at the basket each kid had at their feet. Inside each basket was a pile of sticks and twigs.

"We're collecting wood for the fire tonight," Dan said, answering Lee's question before he even asked it.

"That's right," Sandy added excitedly. "We're meeting a bunch more people up here tonight, and there's going to be a big gathering with all kinds of food and singing and everything."

"You're probably going to have a huge bonfire, too, right?" Lee's mouth turned down with disgust. "Our troop leader won't even let us have one dinky little campfire."

"Our fire will be pretty big, all right," Dan confirmed. "This is the first year my sister and I have been allowed to come, but they have a huge fire every year."

"Who are *they?*" Lee practically growled, angry that he was left out of all the fun. "Your parents?"

"The group they belong to," Dan clarified. "It's called . . . well, we're not allowed to say." He paused uncomfortably for a moment. "Anyway, they come out here every year on the first of May."

"Well," said Lee, abruptly turning away, "I hope you enjoy yourselves."

"We will," Dan said to Lee's retreating back. "You can come, too, if you want."

"Yeah," called Sandy. "Why don't you?"

"Yeah, sure," Lee said without turning around. "Like my troop leader's really gonna let me go."

But as Lee kept walking, he considered the invitation. Then all of a sudden, his whole attitude brightened, and he quickly walked across the field to find Roger and Steve.

Later that night, after the troop wolfed down another boring freeze-dried meal, Mr. Stone sent them all to bed. "We've got a big day of hiking tomorrow," he said cheerfully, "and I want each of you to get a good night's sleep."

Determined more than ever to have a little fun, Lee pulled Steve and Roger aside as they walked toward their tent and told them about the two kids he'd met.

"And they're going to have a really cool fire," Lee went on as the three of them were laying on their sleeping bags, staring out at the night sky. "It's going to be gigantic," he went on, as if he knew what he was talking about.

Then, as if on cue, a bright light appeared in the distance. "There it is!" he exclaimed, pointing at what he was sure was the fire. "Do you guys see that?"

Steve and Roger looked where Lee was pointing. At first it looked like one of the nearby hilltops was glowing eerily. Then, after a moment it became clear that what they were seeing was the blaze from a fire on the other side of the hill. The light from the flames was outlining the rounded top of the hill with an ominous orange glow.

"Are you really going to go check it out?" whispered Steve.

"I said I was, didn't I?" Lee said roughly. He'd told his friends that from the start, and although he had managed to convince Roger to come with him, Steve remained reluctant. "It's not too late to change your mind and come with us, you know."

"You're nuts," Steve whispered. "If Stone catches you guys, you're cooked!"

"How's he going to catch us?" Lee wanted to know. "It's pitch black outside. Besides, he's probably asleep by now. If we're quiet we can get over there and back without anyone ever knowing."

Steve shook his head, but Lee could tell he was weakening.

"What if you get lost?" Steve asked feebly.

"It's the only hill around that looks like it's glowing," Roger pointed out. "How could we miss it?"

"And on the way back," Lee said, thinking fast, "all we have to do is look for that tree—there." He pointed to the huge oak tree in the middle of the clearing. "I'll take a flashlight, and with our compasses it'll be a cinch."

Finally the urging of his friends and the lure of excitement proved to be too much for Steve to resist. "Okay," he said slowly, "I'll come."

Quietly the three friends waited until they heard a huge snore coming from Mr. Stone's tent, then they prepared to leave.

"He's out cold," Lee whispered, stifling a laugh. "Let's go."

"Wait," Steve held back. "What if one of the others hears us? I say we wait until we're sure everyone is asleep."

"The party will be over by then," Lee hissed.

But Steve wouldn't change his mind, and Roger agreed with him.

Fuming, Lee waited with his friends while the camp grew quieter and quieter. Slowly the sounds of whispered conversations and smothered laughter from the other tents faded away. Finally there was no sign of movement, and Lee looked once again at the periodic blinking of his watch.

"Come on, you guys," he whispered. "It's nearly eleven o'clock." He peered through the mesh door of the tent. The glow in the distance was still there. *It's even a little stronger*, Lee thought. *That must be one heck of a fire.*

He carefully unzipped the front flap of the tent, and the boys eased out of the doorway one by one.

"If Stone sees us," Roger whispered, "just tell him we're going to the bathroom."

It was a dumb comment, but the tension made it seem outrageously funny. Biting their cheeks and holding their breath to keep from laughing, the three boys snuck away from the campsite.

When they felt they were safely out of hearing, Steve fell on the ground, curled into a ball, and burst into laughter. Lee and Roger joined in until Lee suddenly turned serious on them.

"Come on, you guys. We're acting like a bunch of clowns," he said with authority as if he had already decided he was in charge of their expedition. "Let's see what's going on up there."

Steve and Roger snapped to attention and saluted Lee, then burst into giggles again. Shaking his head, Lee flashed his penlight on the face of his compass. Then, satisfied that he knew the direction back to camp, he headed for the distant hill.

"Ready, Sergeant Bozo?" Roger asked Steve.

"Ready, Captain Roger," answered Steve. "Shall we follow General Lee?"

"Let's!" exclaimed Roger. And laughing, the two friends took off after their serious buddy, Lee.

Although the hill wasn't actually very far away, walking there in the dark took the boys much longer than it would have during daytime. The pale sliver of a moon, barely shedding enough light to see by, was no help at all. So, given the uncertain light, it was almost no surprise when Roger stepped badly on a large root and crashed to the ground with a yelp of pain.

"What is it?" Lee asked, turning around sharply. He had been in the lead the whole way.

Roger couldn't answer at first, and Lee and Steve could barely make out Roger's body writhing on the ground in pain. Finally he managed to tell them he thought his ankle was broken.

"Can you walk?" asked Steve.

"Could *you* walk on a broken ankle?" Roger snapped.

Lee frowned. "Come on, Rog. It's not broken. You probably just twisted it."

"Oh yeah?" Roger said through clenched teeth. "Let

me twist your ankle like mine is twisted and you can see how it feels!"

"But can you walk?" Steve insisted, bending down to help his friend. "Here, hold on to me."

"It hurts too much!" Roger practically yelped, waving Steve away.

That was enough for Steve. His enthusiasm for their little adventure evaporated like air from a deflating balloon. "Looks like we've got to head back," he said. "Roger's ankle is wasted."

Lee pressed his lips together in frustration. They were almost at the base of the hill. To have come this close and give up really bothered him. Still, it was clear Roger couldn't keep going, and Steve hadn't been that keen on the idea in the first place.

"Tell you what," Lee said to Steve. "Why don't you stay here for a little while with Roger, you know, to give his ankle a chance to get better. In the meantime, I'll climb up the hill real quick and see what's going on. Then I'll come back down to meet you, and we'll all head back to camp together. Okay?"

"Okay," Roger readily agreed, not even wanting to attempt standing up.

Steve shrugged. "Sounds like a plan. But would you at least try to be—"

"Careful," Lee finished for him. "Right. I know." He rolled his eyes. "You sound like my mom." Then, turning quickly, Lee strode off. "See you in a few," he said over his shoulder.

But Lee actually did take Steve's advice. Now that he

was alone, he took special care not to trip or fall over anything, and as a result, it took him over half an hour to reach the base of the hill. From where he stood, the light from the fire was even more obvious than it had been back at camp, and more curious than ever, he began picking his way up to the top. "I'm never going to let those guys live down the fact that they were this close and had to turn back," he said under his breath. "What a couple of wimps!"

The hillside was covered with wet, slippery grass, and dark trees loomed out of the night to spread patches of shadow over Lee, making his ascent that much harder. As he worked his way up and around the summit, he began to hear the sound of voices coming from ahead of him. *It sure sounds like there's a lot of people,* Lee thought, listening to how the voices seemed to rise and fall together as if in a simple rhythm. *Are they chanting?* he wondered.

Pushing ahead, Lee found himself at the edge of a large, level part of the hill. A group of about twenty people stood in a semicircle facing a large bonfire that was burning at the opposite side of the level space, against the hillside. Most of the people, Lee noticed, were dressed in ordinary jeans or shorts, sweatshirts, and T-shirts. But there were three figures wearing brown robes who stood in the center of the group, facing the fire. As Lee entered the area, these robed figures were tossing branches onto the flames.

To the right of the fire was a strangely shaped pile of firewood. Then, looking more closely, Lee realized that it was a human figure made out of sticks and branches. The figure was hollow, as if it were meant to encase something.

"This is really weird," Lee muttered under his breath. But before he could duck back out of sight, Sandy saw him from where she was standing at the edge of the group.

"Hey!" she shouted. "You came!"

Some of the adults turned at Sandy's shout. When they saw Lee, a couple of men started toward him.

Suddenly Lee was overcome with a bad feeling about the whole affair. Beginning to panic, he backed away from the two men, and in the same moment a woman shouted, "Get him!"

The two men leaped at Lee. He tried to dodge their grasp, but felt a strong hand grip his shoulder from behind. Then, suddenly, he was harshly thrown to the ground. "Steve! Rog!" he yelled frantically. "Help!" But he knew they couldn't hear him over the roar and crackle of the fire. Still, he opened his mouth to scream again when something crashed into the side of his head and his vision went black.

The first thing Lee noticed was a warm, orange glow on his eyelids. Then, when he opened his eyes, he saw that he had been brought closer to the fire. Despite the heat that rose off the flames, his sweat-covered body was chilled—especially when he realized he was tied *inside* the hollow branch figure he had seen earlier. His arms and legs were bound to the wooden frame, and there was a gag in his mouth.

One of the robed figures—a bearded man—was standing next to Lee. As soon as he saw Lee's eyes open, he joined the other robed men in front of the fire and they began to chant.

A group of people came over to Lee's cage and stood around it. Lee tried to talk, but couldn't form words through the gag. Still, a woman near his head must have guessed what he was asking.

"This is our annual ritual," she explained. "It's really a celebration of the renewal of sun and of life. And somehow the sacrificial life that we are supposed to offer always seems to gravitate to us. This year *you* are the lucky one who came."

Lucky one! Lee's mind raced in horror as he tried to wriggle out of his ties.

But then all the people, including Dan and Sandy, gathered around his cage, and he was lifted into the air. Slowly they walked closer and closer toward the fire.

"No!!!" Lee screamed, but they couldn't understand him through the gag.

"It's quite an honor to be our sacrifice," the woman whispered in his ear. "The fire—it's beautiful, isn't it?"

Lee's eyes grew wide as what she was saying became clear. Then he almost had to laugh—after all, he'd wanted a fire so badly.

THE END

Greenhouse Effect

$\mathfrak{H}$ALLY HAD BEEN PUTTING OFF HER READING assignment for history class all week long. She hated history, and only the fact that she had a quiz tomorrow finally forced her to drag herself back to her room after dinner and open the dreaded textbook. Then, like a last-minute pardon from the governor, her phone rang.

She snatched up the receiver before the echo of the first ring died away and immediately recognized the voice of her friend Natalie. Although most of the other kids in school thought Natalie was a bit strange, Hally had always gotten along fine with her. True, Natalie could be a little weird sometimes, but Hally actually liked that. She also suspected that she was Natalie's only friend, and she sometimes felt a little sorry for her.

"Are you watching TV?" Natalie asked excitedly.

"I wish," Hally responded, sighing. "I'm studying for the history exam tomorrow. Why?"

"Turn it on . . . oh no. Forget it . . ." Natalie's voice trailed off.

"What?" Hally demanded impatiently.

"Never mind," Natalie said absently. "I'll tell you tomorrow. I've got to study, too. See you."

"Okay," Hally said hesitantly. "See you tomorrow." She stared at the receiver, then hung up the phone. *What was that all about?* she wondered. Then, with a sigh, she turned back to her history book.

The next morning Hally cornered Natalie by her locker before their first class. "So what was on TV last night that was so important?" Hally demanded.

Natalie glanced around at the other students to make sure no one could overhear her. "Well, at first I thought I saw my mom on the screen," she said in a rush, "but it wasn't her. I mean, I'm sure it was her car, but my mom claims it wasn't her in it."

"Natalie," Hally said, holding up a hand to slow her friend down, "what are you talking about?"

Her excited friend took a deep breath and tried to explain. "I was watching that new law show—you know, "Scales of Justice"? Anyway, they had a scene where one of the lawyers is driving down the street. And the car right behind him was my mom's."

"Cool!" Hally exclaimed. "Did your mom know she was being filmed?"

"That's just it," Natalie answered, her voice starting to rise again. "It wasn't my mom driving!"

"Was it your dad?"

"Hally," Natalie scolded, "I wouldn't be this excited if it was just my dad that was driving. No, it was a woman . . . and she looked an awful lot like my mom. I swear, I think she could have been her double."

Hally tried to understand what her friend was so excited about. "So maybe your mom loaned the car to a friend. Does your mom have any friends that look like her?"

Natalie shook her head.

"Or maybe it wasn't even your mom's car at all," Hally ventured. "You could have made a mistake, you know."

"Hally, listen to me," Natalie said, looking her friend sternly in the eye. "First of all, it was *definitely* my mom's car. Same paint job, same broken headlight, same stupid charm thing hanging from the mirror. Second, my mom has never, *ever* loaned her car to anyone. I think she'd rather loan *me* to someone than loan her car! And, if she *had* loaned it, why wouldn't she have said so when I asked her if she was the woman I'd seen?"

Hally frowned. "I still don't see what the big deal is. What are you trying to say, that someone stole—"

"Well, that's just it," Natalie interrupted, all of the excitement draining from her voice. "I don't really know what I'm saying. I just thought it was pretty weird, that's all. Like somebody's been using our stuff without us even being aware of it."

Hally felt a small shiver tickle the back of her neck. *Leave it to Natalie to come up with something weird like that*, she thought. "And your mom was *sure* it wasn't her?" she asked after a moment.

Natalie scowled. "I guess so. Actually she wouldn't really talk to me about it. She was busy with those stupid plants of hers."

Hally nodded. *This* she understood. Natalie's mom owned a nursery that supplied all sorts of exotic plants.

Unfortunately most of the plants demanded constant attention, and Hally often thought Natalie's mom cared more for her plants than she did for Natalie. Hally and her own mother had talked once or twice about it, and it was her mom's opinion that it was this lack of attention that made Natalie act odd sometimes.

"Kids will do just about anything to get attention from their parents," Hally's mom had told her. Then she had grinned and ruffled Hally's hair. "Except perfect ones like you."

Hally smiled at the thought of how great her relationship with her mom was, and felt a twinge of sadness that Natalie and her mom weren't as close. She was just about to offer some words of consolation to her friend when the bell rang for class.

The rest of the day went by quickly, and Hally didn't have a chance to talk to Natalie again. In fact, by the time she got home that night, she had pretty much forgotten her friend's story . . . until the phone rang again while she was reading. She picked up the receiver and heard Natalie whisper her name into the phone.

"Natalie, what's wrong?" she asked, a little worried. "Why are you whispering?"

"I can't talk too loud," her friend continued in a hushed voice. "Listen, I think I've figured out what's going on."

"What do you mean?"

"With the car!" Natalie hissed. "I think it was something *pretending* to be my mother!"

Hally's stomach shifted a little, as if it were preparing itself for some bad news. "Uh, Nat, what do you mean, some*thing*? Don't you mean some*one*?"

Natalie ignored her. "Look, I didn't say anything before because I thought it was just me. But my mom's been acting kind of strange lately—you know, sort of super nice. Anyway, I thought it was because she'd just gotten a whole bunch of new plants in, and she was feeling guilty for spending so much time in the nursery. But now I'm thinking that it's something else. I mean, it's almost like something has taken over her body, something like one of her plants. Hally, her skin even looks a little green!"

Hally's stomach clenched itself into a knot. For the first time in their friendship, she began to wonder if Natalie was completely sane.

"Natalie," she began, while trying to figure out what to say next, "don't you think there's a simpler explanation? Like, maybe your mom isn't feeling well?"

"At first I did, yeah," Natalie whispered urgently. "But get this. When I got home today I found her in the middle of the living room with photos and stuff spread out all over the floor."

"And?" Hally prompted.

"And," Natalie continued, "I asked her what she was doing, and she said she was just reliving some old memories."

"Sounds reasonable to me," Hally answered.

"That's just it!" Natalie exclaimed. "My mom is the most unsentimental person alive. About two months ago she was going to throw all that stuff out, and my dad had to convince her to keep it. Why would she suddenly be so interested in looking through it all unless she was trying to learn something about herself?"

Hally tried to figure out what she could say that would calm her friend down. Her first thought was that maybe Natalie's mom had found out she was dying. That would explain why she was going over her past and being extra nice to Natalie. It would even explain why her color looked a bit funny. But how could she say that to Natalie? Terrified she would say the wrong thing, Hally finally told Natalie to try to get some rest. "Look, Nat," she said, "a good night's sleep will do you good, and in the morning we'll figure something out."

"Sleep?" Natalie softly shrieked. "Are you nuts? With my mom—I mean, that *thing* in the house?"

Hally's mind raced. "Sure. You have to pretend everything is normal, right? Or else your mom—*it*—will know that you know something's up, and then you'll *really* be in trouble."

Natalie was silent for a moment, and Hally wondered if she had said the right thing. "Yeah," Natalie finally whispered, "you're right. I'll have to act like nothing's going on. Okay. Thanks, Hally."

"No problem," Hally said, convinced her friend had gone off the deep end. "I'll see you tomorrow."

After hanging up, Hally began to cry. She didn't know what to do. She knew that she should say something to her parents, but she was afraid of what would happen to Natalie. *What if they put her away?* she thought, trying to erase the images of white rooms and straitjacketed patients that filled her mind.

On the other hand, Hally was also afraid of what would happen to Natalie if she *didn't* tell someone. Finally she decided that she would see how her friend was in the morning, and if she hadn't come to her senses, Hally would convince Natalie to see the school counselor.

But the next day Natalie didn't show up for class, and Hally found herself hardly able to sit still as she anxiously waited for the final bell to ring. When it did, she bolted out of her seat like she'd gotten an electric shock and raced toward Natalie's house.

A plan had formed in Hally's mind while she had squirmed through her long schoolday, and now she definitely had decided to carry it out.

If Natalie's home, then I'll try to talk some sense into her, Hally told herself. *At least I'll try to get her to talk to someone else about all this besides me.*

But what Hally could barely admit to herself was the scary thought that Natalie might *not* be home—that she had done something crazy like run away. If that were the case, Hally didn't know what she'd do. Maybe she'd even have to consider talking to Natalie's mother about it.

When she reached Natalie's house, Hally rang the bell. After waiting a few minutes, she tried it again, then tried knocking a few times. Then, just as she was about to give up, Natalie's mom came to the door.

"Uh, hi, Mrs. Porter," Hally said nervously. She caught herself looking for a greenish tinge in the woman's skin. "Is Natalie home?"

Natalie's mom looked confused. "Why do you ask?"

Hally looked at her feet. *So Natalie wasn't home. Now what could she say?* "Because," she finally answered, "because, well, actually, I really need to talk to you. Would it be all right if I came in for a moment?"

Mrs. Porter smiled broadly and opened the door. Hally stepped into the living room and tried to think of a good way to tell Natalie's mother that her daughter was crazy. "I'm not exactly sure how to say this, Mrs. Porter," she began, "but have you noticed anything funny about Natalie lately?"

"Funny? How do you mean?" Mrs. Porter asked.

"Well, like . . . like if she didn't seem to trust you or want to be near you," Hally finally blurted out.

Mrs. Porter crossed her arms and regarded Hally with genuine curiosity. "Perhaps you had better tell me what you're getting at."

Hally shifted uncomfortably. "Well, you see, Natalie called me the other night and she was saying some pretty . . . um, strange things about you."

Hally went on to describe, as kindly as possible, the outburst of her friend and the things Natalie had said about her mother. She finished by saying, "I was going to try to talk to Natalie some more today at school, but she didn't show up. So I thought I'd better come over here and see if everything was all right."

Natalie's mom listened carefully to every word of Hally's story and seemed to take the news rather calmly. Instead of yelling or getting angry, she simply smiled faintly and shook her head.

"Thank you for your concern," she said after a moment, "but I already knew most of this. You see, Natalie and I had a long talk last night—I assume it was after she spoke to you."

Hally felt the faint stirring of hope inside her. "And is everything all right?"

"Now it is, yes," Natalie's mom said. "Now, since I've decided to divide my time more evenly between Natalie and my plants. In fact, that's why she missed school today—we spent the day together in the nursery."

Hally's tiny hope expanded and showed itself on her face in a wide grin. "That's great!" she exclaimed. "I hope you're not mad at me for butting in."

"Not at all," Mrs. Porter responded warmly. "I'm glad to know Natalie has someone to confide in."

Hally couldn't stop herself from grinning as she turned toward the door. "Well, when Natalie gets home, tell her to give me a call, okay?"

"Oh," Mrs. Porter said, holding out a hand to stop Hally, "Natalie's home. She's out back in the greenhouse."

"Really?" Hally asked, thinking how Natalie always said she'd had enough of those stupid plants and never wanted to go out there. In fact, she'd never even taken Hally out to see it. "Can I go see her?"

"Certainly," Natalie's mom said happily. "Let me take you."

Mrs. Porter led Hally through the house to the backyard, which was filled with tropical trees, sweet-scented flowers, dark green vines, and lush ferns. They pushed their way through the miniature jungle to the door of the greenhouse, where Mrs. Porter motioned Hally inside.

Whereas the garden had smelled wonderfully sweet, the scent in the greenhouse was nearly overpowering. Right next to the door was an enormous plant with thick, pink buds. At the top of the plant was an open flower that seemed to wave gently in the breeze coming through the open door.

Hally stopped next to this enormous plant and looked around in wonder, then turned to Mrs. Porter. "Where's Natalie?" she asked.

"Behind you," Mrs. Porter said matter-of-factly.

Hally turned around in confusion and bent to look around the large plant that stood next to her. Then, at that moment, she felt something sharp prick her in the neck. "Ouch," she said, bringing her hand up to swat at whatever it was. She felt something thin and sticky clinging to her neck and jerked her head back to see what was on her.

That's when she saw a white, ropy tendril coming from the plant by the door. Apparently it had snaked out of the odd plant and slapped onto her neck.

"Yuck!" Hally exclaimed, tugging at the gummy tendril, but she couldn't get it loose from her skin. Growing terrified, she turned to say something to the oddly calm Mrs. Porter, but when she tried to move, Hally found she suddenly had no control over her body. In fact, she felt like she was floating outside of herself. Then, without warning, her body slumped to the floor and her head fell against the horrible plant that had hold of her.

Spreading quickly through her body, the plant's poison numbed her vocal cords and froze her mouth, keeping her from screaming when she saw what was concealed behind the monster plant. It was Natalie—or the shell of her body, now thickly covered with roots.

With great effort, for the poison was now spreading fast through every inch of her body, Hally turned her eyes toward Mrs. Porter, and saw that the once kind expression on the woman's face had turned into an evil grin.

"You shouldn't 'plant' your nose where it doesn't belong," the horrible woman said, letting out a low chuckle of delight as she turned to walk out of the greenhouse.

Looking up as the room went dim, Hally saw the last sight of her life. There, growing from the plant that loomed above her head, was one of its huge, pink buds . . . and it seemed to be molding itself into the outline of a little girl.

THE END

A "True" Story

$\Longrightarrow\ \cdot\ \longleftrightarrow\ \cdot\ \ominus\ \cdot\ \longleftrightarrow\ \cdot\ \longleftarrow$

MARK TOSSED THE BRANCH HE HAD BEEN playing with onto the fire. "All right," he said to the other students, "I've got one."

Mark and his classmates were on the annual Keystone Middle School's spring trip. This year the class had elected to go camping in the forested mountains of the Colorado Rockies. They had piled into a school bus early in the morning and had driven most of the day to reach the campground, now dotted with multicolored tent domes.

Although there were two teachers along for supervision, the boys who had been lucky enough to come were mostly left on their own. The teachers' tents were off to one side, far enough away to give the students the feeling of independence. Now, Mark and his buddies were taking advantage of their freedom by staying up long after the teachers had gone to bed and sitting around the campfire, trying to terrify each other with scary stories.

Kurt and Felix had already told some pretty petrifying ones, but Mark felt sure his would really rattle their wits. "I won't tell you how I heard about this," he began, his face eerily lit by the dancing flames of the fire, "but I will promise that what I'm about to tell you is a true story."

Kurt snorted, but was promptly hushed by the others. They had a "golden rule," which stated that each storyteller had to be given a fair chance, so Mark just ignored Kurt and began.

"There was this kid," he said in a hushed tone. "We'll call him Mike. He lived alone with his dad at the edge of town, real close to the forest where his dad worked as a lumberjack.

"Sometimes Mike's dad would be gone for a few days when he was working deep in the forest, so Mike learned how to take care of himself. He wasn't afraid of the woods like a lot of the other kids. In fact, he was always goofing around among the huge trees, setting traps and fishing and stuff. Pretty soon, he knew his way around the woods better than most anyone else.

"Anyway, one night while his dad was gone, Mike was sitting out on his front porch. He was staring up at the sky through his telescope when all of a sudden he saw a falling star. He watched it shoot across the sky, and then he realized he could track it with his telescope. He was following the fiery blaze, watching it fall closer and closer to earth, when it actually got close enough that he didn't need his scope anymore to see it. In fact, it was getting so near to him that he could feel the heat . . . especially since it was coming right at him!"

"Bam!" yelled Kurt, clapping his hands together sharply.

The boy sitting next to him jumped, and everyone else laughed and poked the poor guy in the ribs. Then Felix, the class science nerd, had to step in and ruin the mood.

"You know that's not really possible," Felix said. "Actually a shooting star is most likely to—"

"Fee-lix!" the other boys shouted him down. "Nobody wants a science lecture now."

"Are you guys through?" Mark said, pretending to be the adult in the group. He waited for everybody to settle down, then resumed his story.

"When Mike saw this thing flaming down out of the sky, he jumped for cover—and just in time. The meteor slammed into the ground about a hundred yards away. There was a huge flash of light and the sound of hundreds of trees snapping like pencils. Then everything got real quiet.

"Well, Mike didn't wait a single second. He took off running toward where he had seen the thing come down. But it was weird—there were no flames in sight. Still, it wasn't hard to find. All he had to do was follow the smell—not of fire, but of something like burning rubber.

"Within minutes, he reached the crash site. It was awesome. The trees were all smashed up like twigs, and in the middle of the clearing was this huge pile of dirt that had been pushed up like a wave. Smoke was coming from the dirt, and Mike decided to get closer for a better look at what he was sure was a meteor.

"Except it wasn't a meteor. It was something silvery that kind of glowed in the dark." Mark paused for a moment, then said practically in a whisper, "It was a spaceship."

Felix guffawed. "Yeah, right. And you said this was a *true* story."

Once again everyone chorused "Fee-lix!" until the bespectacled future scientist gave up and let Mark go on with his story.

"Well, needless to say, Mike couldn't believe what he saw," Mark began again. "So he slid down the pile of dirt until he was actually standing on the ship itself. The surface was shiny, smooth, and warm to the touch. Mike figured a lot of it was buried underground since it didn't look very big.

"Anyway, he was standing there, wondering what to do, when suddenly he heard a faint knocking sound. At first he thought it was the sound of the surface of the ship cooling, but then he realized that it was coming from *inside*. The knocking grew louder, and then—*Crack!*—a big gash opened up in the metal hull!"

Everybody flinched and the guy that Kurt had scared earlier gave a tiny yelp. The others teased him unmercifully, but Mark knew they were just trying to laugh off their own fright. He jumped up and started to walk around as he continued telling his story.

"The crack grew wider and wider until it made a circular hole. Then a horrible smell rolled out of the opening—it reminded Mike of the time he had found a rotting rabbit in a forgotten trap. It stunk so bad, Mike's legs went all rubbery, and he was shaking so much he could barely stand.

"Finally the crack stopped getting wider, so Mike inched his way closer to what was obviously some kind of doorway. His heart pounded so hard it practically made his shirt jump up and down, and the night seemed very quiet all of a sudden. He reached the edge of the opening and slowly leaned forward. Inch by inch, his head poked over the edge. He licked his lips, now dry with fear and excitement. He was going to be famous. He was going to be the first human ever to meet an alien!"

Mark looked around at his audience. He really had them, but knew he'd better get to the scary part soon. He went on, trying to make his voice sound ominous and spooky.

"First Mike saw some blinking lights on the inside wall. Next, he saw something that looked like a tunnel into the center of the ship. He leaned a little farther . . . and there it was—a dark shape lying in the middle of the tunnel.

"Suddenly a tentacle shot out! Before Mike could scream, it wrapped around his throat. He tried to get away, but the slimy thing was too strong for him. Gasping for breath, he felt himself being pulled over the edge of the hole and into the ship. The thing—a hideous cross between a spider and an octopus—had him . . . and it was pulling him closer to its mouth!"

Mark held his hands about a foot apart. "Mike was this close to going down the gross thing's ugly, slimy throat. In fact, he was so close he almost passed out from the stench of the thing's breath. Then its tongue—with millions of tiny teeth right on it—snaked out. It swirled across Mike's face like sandpaper, tearing into his cheeks and practically ripping off his nose. Then, just before he blacked out, Mike saw small tentacles ooze out of the alien's head. Although he tried, he couldn't fight off the alien as it sank one of its tentacles right into his skull and bored through it like it was a coconut, heading straight for his brain."

Mark paused while his audience made appropriate sounds of disgust. Then, before they had time to speak, he held up his hand.

"Wait a minute. There's more. You see, some time later Mike woke up. But he wasn't exactly *Mike* anymore. The alien had taken over, or assimilated, his body . . . *and* his life."

"What?" one of the boys gasped.

"That's right. Once it was comfortable in its new body, the alien set the ship to self-destruct. Then it followed Mike's memories back to the house where he had grown up. There it waited for its new human parent—Mike's dad—to return.

"And the worst part of the whole story is that poor Mike, even though he didn't have a body anymore, still had enough consciousness to know what was happening. He figured out that the alien would take over his dad, too; and that the more humans it assimilated, the more capable it was of reproducing itself over and over again. In time it would control the planet. And all Mike could do was watch in silent horror, knowing that he had brought about the doom of the human race."

Mark's voice dropped to a whisper as he finished, and he stood still in the flickering shadows cast by the waning campfire. The stunned silence was everything he could have hoped for. He waited as his classmates slowly began breathing again.

A boy named Malcolm sighed heavily. "It's like that movie where the scientists are at the South Pole and they find an alien that takes people over and makes copies of them." The boy shivered. "Afterward, the scientists couldn't tell who was real and who was a copy."

Kurt rolled his eyes. Of course *he* had to be the one to try to knock Mark's story down. Kurt was always the first to have something negative to say.

"I thought you said it was a true story," he accused. "That story was no more true than a fairy tale."

Mark looked at him innocently. "It *is* true."

Kurt shook his head. "Uh uh. No way."

Mark tried not to smile. Someone just had to figure it out. In fact, he had been betting on it. "Okay, smart guy," he challenged Kurt, "why is there no way it can be true?"

"There's no way because there was nobody around when the kid went into the spaceship," Kurt said, pouncing on what he was sure was the flaw in Mark's logic. "And if the kid never came out, and the alien blew up the ship, then there's nobody to tell the story and no evidence that the ship or the alien ever existed."

"That's true," Mark admitted. "But you missed one important point."

Everyone listened closely to see how he would defend himself.

"There *is* one person who knows the whole story," Mark said, nearly whispering, "but his name isn't Mike."

Suddenly Mark pulled open his shirt. "It's me!" he yelled as thick, black tentacles shot out from his chest.

Everyone screamed. It looked like a grenade had exploded in the middle of the circle as the boys jumped, crawled, or rolled backward away from the monster who

had once been Mark.

"What is it?" yelled the teachers as they came racing over from their tents.

Mark knelt in front of the fire, nearly breathless with laughter. Tears streamed down his face as he propped himself with his hands to keep from falling over. The tentacles now bounced and swayed gently at his side, looking suspiciously like black nylons stuffed with something springy.

"What's going on?" demanded Mr. Owens, the English teacher.

Mark managed to catch his breath and tried to answer, but the sight of his classmates slowly picking themselves up made him break out laughing once again.

"Ah, nothing, Mr. Owens," said Mark's best friend, Zack, who had kept quiet throughout Mark's story.

"Nothing?" repeated Mr. DeRocha, the science teacher. "You were all screaming like it was the end of the world!"

Mark finally recovered enough to talk. "We were telling scary stories, and I guess mine was a little too scary."

The teachers—hands on hips—studied the group of kids. Everyone was trying to look as if it had been somebody else screaming and not them.

Finally Mr. Owens pronounced that it was late and that everyone had to be in their tents—*asleep*—within the next fifteen minutes.

Most of the kids were still too embarrassed to do anything but agree. Some of them shot Mark dirty looks, but others grinned or gave him the thumbs-up sign, wishing they had been as clever as he was.

True to Mr. Owens's wishes, fifteen minutes later

everyone was in their tents, although not exactly asleep. The sound of whispered conversations and muffled laughter could be heard from every tent.

"Geez," Zack said in a low voice from his side of the dark tent he and Mark shared, "you nailed us all with that one."

Mark smiled. "You know, I think Nigel almost had a heart attack."

Zack clutched his chest and fell backward. The two boys burst into giggles and spent the next few minutes making jokes about who had been the most scared of the group.

After their laughing fit had passed, Zack asked Mark quietly, "Where did you get that story from, anyway?"

"Why?" Mark whispered.

"I mean, did you get it from that movie Malcolm was talking about?"

"What makes you think I made it up?" Mark asked, suddenly serious.

Zack was silent a moment. Then he said in an angry tone, "Come on, Mark. I really want to know where you got the story. Stop goofing around."

Mark didn't answer right away. The silence in the tent seemed to take on a life of its own. Finally the breath Mark had been holding in exploded out of his mouth in a bark of laughter. "Of course I made it up! What do you think—it really happened?"

There was a strange sound from Zack, as if his sleeping bag was being torn open. "Good," he sneered as he clamped a hand tightly over Mark's mouth. "I was worried for a moment that I'd been discovered."

THE END

Judgment Day

WELL, WHAT DO YOU GUYS WANT TO DO?" asked Alex.

He and his friends Sarah and John were sitting around the living room of his family's cabin, staring lazily at the fire. Everyone's parents were across the dirt road at a party being given by Sarah's mom and dad. That left Alex and his friends to themselves. But, to Alex's disgust, nobody seemed to want to do anything.

"We could play a game," John suggested.

Alex shook his head. After years of coming up to the cabin, he'd played all the games stored away in the musty old closets. But then he remembered there was one game he hadn't tried.

"How about trying to summon a spirit with the Ouija board?" he asked the others.

John laughed. "You've got to be kidding. Ouija boards are stupid."

"Why?" demanded Alex defensively.

"Oh, come on," John scoffed. "Nobody believes in those things. Someone's always pushing around the pointer to try to scare the other players."

"I heard that they work sometimes," countered Sarah. "I vote we try it. Besides, it's the perfect game for this kind of night." She glanced at the torrents of rain streaming down the windowpane. "Just look at that lightning."

Alex looked at the window, then back at John. "Sarah's right. It's the perfect night for a Ouija board. Maybe the lights will even go out. Come on, John. It'll be fun."

John finally caved in, and Alex ran upstairs to his room to get the board. He had found it yesterday when he was poking around in the attic. His parents didn't like him to go up there—the place was jammed with all kinds of stuff that could topple down on somebody—but he was bored stiff and had to find something to do. Besides, the attic was a cool place to explore. The cabin had been in Alex's family for generations, and each generation left something interesting behind. Alex had found everything from old cowboy hats to Halloween masks. But his favorite find was the old photo album. His great-grandfather had been a sheriff, and there were some really neat photographs of the stately gentleman standing outside his jail, a long rifle in his hand and a glint in his eyes.

"Here it is," Alex announced, returning with the mildewed cardboard box. He and his friends gathered in a circle in front of the fireplace, and Alex set the board on the pine floorboards.

"Okay," said Alex, "we have to promise not to move the pointer ourselves."

"Says here it's called a *planchette*," said John, reading the box.

"Fine," said Alex. "Let's all promise not to move the planchette."

"Sure," said John.

"I promise," said Sarah.

Satisfied, Alex placed the heart-shaped pointer, which was made of plastic with a clear circle in the center, on the slick board. Feeling a little foolish, he gently rested his fingertips on the outer rim of the pointer and motioned for John and Sarah to do the same.

"Now what?" asked John in a hushed voice.

"I think we're supposed to ask it something," said Alex, "but what, I don't know."

"I thought we were supposed to try and contact someone," Sarah said.

"Let's just sit here for a minute and see what happens," John suggested, getting into the mood.

They sat in silence, their fingers resting on the smooth plastic pointer as the ancient grandfather clock ticked away minute after minute.

Finally, after five minutes, Alex broke the tension. "Uh, hello out there," he called. "Is anybody listening? Can anybody hear me?"

The three kids sat perfectly still, the only sound coming from the crackling logs in the fireplace. Then, all at once, the air in the room seemed to become strained, as if the night was pressing on the walls of the cabin. Three pairs of eyes stared at the board with its selection of numbers and letters.

Alex's heart was suddenly beating faster. He could feel his arms beginning to tremble with the strain of holding his fingers just on the surface of the planchette. He couldn't stand it, and just as he was about to lift his hands, the pointer moved.

Although his back was to the fire, Alex felt as if a freezing wind had just blown down his shirt. He looked wide-eyed at the others. They were obviously as shocked as he was.

Then the pointer moved again, this time taking a tiny jerk to the left.

"Who's doing that?" John asked in a strangled whisper.

"Not me," said Sarah.

"Me neither," Alex breathed.

The planchette moved again, a little more forcefully. Almost as if it was gaining confidence, it slid farther toward the left of the board, then stopped abruptly.

"Quick," said Alex, recovering slightly, "what letter is it over?"

"Looks like the O," said Sarah, leaning over and peering through the small oval window.

"Could be the N," John pointed out.

"Keep your hands still," Alex warned.

Before they could definitely determine which letter appeared in the little window, the pointer was off again, now moving much more smoothly as it slid to the right and down. But when it stopped there was nothing in the window. It stood halfway between the bottom row of letters and the row of numbers.

"What's that mean?" asked Sarah.

She gave a little shriek as the pointer suddenly jumped to the right and up, then quickly over to the left. Finally, it came back to rest in the center between the numbers and letters.

Sarah took her fingers off the planchette and pushed herself away from the board. "All right," she said in a shaky voice, "who did that? It's *not* funny!"

Alex sat back, too. "It wasn't me, I swear. It almost moved out from under my fingertips."

"Oh, this is stupid!" John scoffed. "There is no such thing as spirits. And even if there were, why would they hang around waiting for someone to use a Ouija board to bring them back? Besides, if we are talking to a spirit he or she isn't making much sense."

Alex had to agree. "I read somewhere that the nerves in our fingers make the planchette move," he said. "I know my arms were getting pretty tired trying to keep my hands still."

"Make up your mind," Sarah said in a high voice. "A minute ago you were saying that the pointer moved all on its own." She paused to take a deep breath. "So? Do you guys think we contacted anybody?"

"Well," Alex said slowly, "I've been studying the board. If we did, it was trying to leave a message I can't figure out. The first letter was an N or an O. After that there was a blank, then what looked like a W. Then came another N or an O, and a blank again."

John smirked. "Brilliant. Maybe we made contact with a ghost that can't spell!" He chuckled. "I don't know about you guys, but contacting the dead always makes me hungry."

Sarah laughed, and even Alex had to smile. He put the board back in its box.

"Let's make some S'mores," Sarah suggested.

Her idea met with enthusiastic approval, and they spent the rest of the evening gorging themselves on the gooey chocolate-and-marshmallow treats, completely avoiding the subject of Ouija boards and ghosts.

But later that night, long after John's and Sarah's parents had picked them up and Alex and his parents had gone to bed, Alex couldn't sleep. He knew for a fact that *he* had not been moving the pointer. In fact, he still vividly remembered how tired his arms had been, and that he was about to lift his fingers off the plastic just before it moved the first time.

Still, that didn't rule out the possibility that one of the others had moved it. He didn't think Sarah had. She seemed too scared by the whole thing. And even though John was skeptical, he seemed to have really gotten into the whole thing.

That left only some kind of spirit or ghost, Alex thought. *Something* had made the planchette move . . . but why wouldn't it send a readable message?

Realizing that he was never going to get any sleep, Alex quietly got up and crept over to his bedroom door. He knew his parents had already gone to bed, but there was no point in taking any chances. He softly closed the door and flipped on the lamp on his nightstand. Then he pulled the Ouija board out from under his bed, slid it out of the box, and placed it on the floor. He set the pointer in the middle and carefully retraced the route it had taken over the board.

Alex sat back and frowned. The letters appearing in the window were completely unconnected. "It doesn't make any sense," he whispered, thinking that John was probably right in the first place—Ouija boards were stupid.

He picked up the odd-looking pointer and looked at it. It was certainly light enough to move on its own, he thought.

And then an idea hit him. Quickly setting the pointer back onto the board, Alex once again traced the route it had taken earlier. But this time he looked at the letters at the pointed end of the planchette, not in the window.

"A-T-L-A-S-T," he murmured. Alex sat back and clenched his arms across his chest to fight the shivers that swept through him. *"At last,"* he said, trembling with fear and excitement as he remembered how he had asked if anybody could hear him. Now it was obvious that someone—or some*thing*—had. And it must have been waiting to be called on for a long time.

Alex tried to swallow, but his mouth and throat were completely dry. He stared at the yellowed board as if it were a coiled rattlesnake, ready to strike. Then, slowly, carefully, he scooted closer. He reached over and slid the pointer back to the center of the board and stared at it a while longer.

Finally, not quite believing what he was doing, he placed his fingers on the planchette. "Are you still there?" Alex whispered.

Nothing happened, and feeling oddly relieved, Alex let out a deep sigh. Then, just before he lifted his fingers, the pointer seemed to twitch. Alex gasped, and his heart hammered madly as the pointer slid gracefully around the board.

"D-O-N-T-B-E-S-C-A-R-E-D," Alex numbly spelled out the letters it made. "Don't be scared—good advice," he said, laughing weakly. "Except it's coming from a ghost." Gulping hard, he whispered, "Who are you?"

The planchette seemed to gain control of its movements with every second. In reply to Alex's question, it glided from letter to letter as if it were writing.

"K-E-R-W-I-N," Alex spelled out. "Okay, Kerwin," he said, slightly less afraid, "why are you talking to me?"

The planchette pointed out I-A-M-L-O-N-E-L-Y.

Alex could barely sit still. Wait until he told the others. The board had actually worked! But in his excitement, Alex accidentally let his hands slip off the planchette. Suddenly he felt a strange sensation, like the air had been sucked out of the room. He quickly set his fingers back on the plastic pointer, but it didn't move.

"Sorry," Alex whispered when, after a while, nothing had happened. "I'll try again tomorrow."

He stowed the board back under his bed, switched off the light, and slipped under the covers. Exhausted, he fell right to sleep.

᠅ ᠅ ᠅

The next morning, Alex rushed downstairs to find his parents already sitting at the breakfast table.

"Your dad and I are going for a hike this morning now that the storm has cleared up," his mom said. "Why don't you come along?"

"No thanks," Alex said, barely looking up as he wolfed down his breakfast. "I'm going to get together with Sarah and John today and just goof around."

He waited impatiently for his parents to leave, then raced across the road to Sarah's cabin. Her mother told him that Sarah had gone into town with her father and wouldn't be back for an hour or two. Alex thanked her and returned to his cabin to call John.

"John!" he shouted when his friend picked up the phone. "You've got to come over here right now."

"Why?" John asked, obviously startled by the tone of Alex's voice. "What's up?"

"The board—it worked last night! We were reading the letters in the window, but the ghost was pointing at the letters instead!"

"What are you talking about?" John demanded.

"Remember when I asked if anyone could hear us? Well, the message the ghost was trying to get across was 'at last.' And when I tried the Ouija board again, I actually contacted the same spirit again. His name is Kerwin."

There was a long moment of silence. "Yeah, right," John said sarcastically.

"I'm serious!" Alex insisted. "Come over and we'll talk to him together."

"Kerwin, huh? What kind of a name is that?" John said, still sarcastic, but obviously a little curious.

"How would I know?" Alex's voice rose as he became frustrated. "Look, are you coming over or not?"

John thought about it. "Nah, I don't think so. I just got this new game for my computer and—"

"You don't believe me, do you?" Alex said flatly.

"Well, not really," admitted John.

"Fine," Alex said angrily. "I'll just contact Kerwin myself." He slammed the phone down, stomped back upstairs to his room, and drew the Ouija board out from under his bed. Taking it downstairs, he set it on the dining table. Then he placed the pointer on the board. As soon as his hands were on the pointer it moved.

"D-O-N-T-L-E-A-V-E-A-L-E-X," it spelled.

"Cool, you know my name," said Alex. "Tell me more about yourself, Kerwin."

"I-L-I-V-E-D-H-E-R-E."

"Where?" asked Alex.

"Y-O-U-R-C-A-B-I-N."

"Wow!" exclaimed Alex. "How did you die?"

"M-U-R-D-E-R."

A thrill rippled through Alex. This was even better than he had imagined. This ghost was probably trying to get somebody to avenge its death!

"Do you know who did it?" Alex asked, speaking slowly and clearly so Kerwin would understand.

The pointer slid over the word "yes" in the upper left-hand corner. Alex imagined he could feel the tense excitement of the dead man. There was a long pause, and the pointer didn't move.

"Well?" Alex asked impatiently. "Who was it?"

"S-H-E-R-I-F-F."

The answer was so unexpected that Alex rocked back, nearly releasing the planchette. He stared stupidly at the board for a few moments before saying half-aloud, "The sheriff killed you?"

As the planchette slowly moved over the word "yes" again, Alex got a sick feeling in his stomach. "When?" he asked, his voice beginning to tremble.

"1-8-7-9."

Alex felt his world beginning to close in around him.

That was the date on the back of his great-grandfather's photograph. Too scared to move, all Alex could do was read the letters as they slid under the pointer.

"F-I-N-A-L-L-Y-R-E-V-E-N-G-E."

"What?" Alex croaked. "What do you mean?"

The planchette literally flew around the board, and Alex found he couldn't remove his fingers.

"Y-O-U-R-G-R-A-N-D-F-A-T-H-E-R-T-O-O-K-M-Y-L-I-F-E-I-W-I-L-L-N-O-W-T-A-K-E-Y-O-U-R-S."

"No!" Alex yelled, wrenching his fingers away.

But it didn't matter—the planchette no longer needed him. Deliberately, it moved slowly across the board by itself.

"L-O-O-K-B-E-H-I-N-D-Y-O-U," it carefully spelled out.

His flesh beginning to crawl, Alex slowly looked over his shoulder. There, with a noose still around his neck, stood a horrible-looking man dressed in dusty old western clothing. The evil man carefully slipped the rope off his own neck and stepped toward Alex. "The name's Kerwin," the man said, a terrible grin creeping across his weathered face. "I've already met your great-grandpa. So glad to finally have the chance to meet you."

THE END

Bugged

><+>•Θ•<+>•<

"**I** CAN'T BELIEVE IT!" STACY SAID, BARGING INTO her best friend's house. "Wade and some of his friends are going camping—on their own. I *never* get to do things on my own!"

Fawn closed the door and allowed her friend to stomp around the room for a moment. Then she calmly pointed out that Wade had just turned sixteen and could already drive. "Besides," Fawn asked, "since when have *you* been interested in camping?"

"The point is, I'm just as responsible as Wade is," Stacy declared. "*Twice* as responsible!"

Fawn bit back a smile. Stacy and her brother had a very stormy relationship—nothing like the friendly one she had with her older sister, Mattie. Anyway, Fawn knew that nothing she could say would make Stacy feel better, so she just shrugged and stayed silent. And then she had an idea. "Why don't you ask your parents if we could go if my sister came along to watch us?"

Stacy stopped scowling and looked at her friend. "Do you think Mattie would do it?"

Fawn grinned. "I think she might. I know she likes to go camping, and I don't think she's doing anything this weekend."

Stacy's mood instantly changed. "That would be great! Find out if she'll do it first. If she says yes, then I'll ask my mom and dad."

The next day Stacy was in the field behind her house studying a colony of ants swarming all over a dead cockroach, when she heard Fawn calling her from the front of the house. Standing up and brushing the dirt from her jeans, Stacy waved to her friend, who was picking her way across the field of tumbled earth.

"What are you doing?" Fawn called as she came within earshot.

"Watching some ants," Stacy replied. Then she quickly changed the subject. "Did you ask your sister?"

Fawn nodded and broke into a huge grin. "She said yes!"

"All right!" Stacy yelled, then danced a little victory dance with her friend. "Now comes the really hard part— getting my parents to say yes."

"No problem," Fawn predicted confidently. "We're on a roll. Why not talk to your mom now?"

Stacy considered this. "Nah, she's grading some papers. I'll ask her after dinner, when she's more relaxed. Then she can help me convince my dad."

"Sounds like a plan," Fawn said. "Call me later and let me know what happens."

As it turned out, Stacy's parents seemed pretty agreeable to the whole plan—especially when she neglected to mention it was Fawn's idea and indicated that it was Mattie's.

"Actually," Stacy lied, "Mattie's been wanting to go camping for a while. She's got the whole trip planned out, but I said I'd have to ask you guys first." She looked pleadingly at her mother.

"Oh, I didn't realize it was *Mattie's* idea," her mom said, stifling a smile. "Where does *Mattie* want to go camping?"

Stacy paused. She hadn't thought it through that far and didn't really know the names of any campgrounds in the area except for the one where her brother was going. "Rock Hollow," she finally said, hoping her parents hadn't noticed her delayed response.

"What a coincidence," said Stacy's dad, looking at her mom and smiling. Then he shrugged. "Well, if it's all right with your mom, it's okay with me—especially since Wade will be up there this weekend, too."

"Up where?" asked Stacy's brother, coming into the living room. Stacy clenched her teeth—her jerky older brother could ruin everything.

"Stacy, Fawn, and Mattie were thinking of going up to Rock Hollow this weekend," their dad announced. "Your mother and I are thinking it'll be okay since you'll be up there, too."

"What?!" Wade said, obviously shocked. "Well, don't expect *me* to baby-sit them."

"We don't need you to baby-sit us," Stacy shot back.

"No one's asking you to, Wade," their mom said calmly.

"Great," Wade said, throwing his hands in the air as he turned and left the room.

Stacy's father looked at her. "Mattie's how old again?"

"Sixteen," Stacy answered. "Same as Wade."

"Mattie's a responsible girl," Stacy's mom interjected. "As far as I'm concerned they can go." She looked sternly at Stacy. "But I want to know exactly where you intend to camp and exactly when you plan to come back—*and* I want to examine everything you pack before you go."

Stacy was so happy she would have agreed to anything. "Thanks, Mom! Thanks, Dad!" she called over her shoulder, already halfway up the stairs on her way to call Fawn.

✳ ✳ ✳

The next day the trip was set, and by mid-morning on Saturday Stacy, Fawn, and Mattie were pulling into the entrance of Rock Hollow in Mattie's beat-up Volkswagen Bug. From where they parked, the three girls hiked in for at least two hours.

Finally Mattie stopped in a clearing under some tall pine trees. "Home sweet home for the next two days," she declared. "Unless you'd like to go back," she added with a straight face.

"No way," Fawn said, shrugging off her pack and throwing herself to the ground. "I'm beat."

"Me too," gasped Stacy. She took off her pack. "I'm not moving another inch—not after all it took to get here." She slapped her hand against her neck. "Oh, wonderful. We've got fellow campers—mosquitoes."

"Did you know there are over 2,600 species of mosquito?" Fawn asked, sounding like Miss Science.

Stacy scowled at her, then turned to Mattie. "Is your sister always so helpful?" she asked sarcastically.

"Yeah, she's full of useless information," Mattie said. "But as much as I'd like to hear more fascinating information about mosquitoes, we have to set up camp."

And with that, the three girls went to work assembling their tents—one for Mattie and one for Stacy and Fawn. Then they sorted out their cooking gear and began gathering firewood.

When they were finished, they each wolfed down a sandwich they had brought, and Mattie announced that she was going to read for a while.

Stacy and Fawn stared at each other for a long moment, then burst out laughing when it became obvious that neither of them had a clue as to what they were supposed to do. Neither had gone camping before, and now that they were here they really felt kind of, well, lost.

Mattie rolled her eyes. "What a couple of goons." She positioned herself against a tree and opened her book. "Listen, there's plenty of daylight left. You guys are on your own for a while. Why don't you go exploring or something?"

"Good idea," Stacy said.

Fawn agreed, getting to her feet. "Maybe we can find some wildflowers," she suggested.

"These woods can get kind of tricky," Mattie warned. She stretched and yawned. "Don't go too far."

"We won't," Fawn replied as she and Stacy wandered off.

For a while, they walked along in silence, with Fawn stopping to look at nearly every flower they came across.

"Wow," she said in awe, "it's really beautiful up here."

Stacy nodded absently, more interested in searching for signs of animal life. After a while, though, she began to think that the only animal life she was going to find were the relatives of the mosquito she'd killed earlier. It seemed like every two seconds she'd hear that high-pitched whine in her ear, and it was driving her crazy.

"Aargh!" she yelled, waving her hands around her head. "I'm sick of these things!"

"It must be all the rain we had this year," Fawn said. "Mosquitoes like a moist area to lay their eggs."

Stacy turned an angry glare on her friend. "How do you know so much about mosquitoes?" she demanded.

"I did a paper on them for science class last year. Remember how they got to be so bad, everyone in town was talking about spraying the whole countryside with insecticide?"

Stacy did remember. That had been a horrible spring, and she had spent as much time as she could indoors. "Well, it looks like they're going to be just as bad this year," she predicted. "And it looks like just about all of them are breeding at Rock Hollow." She laughed. "I hope Wade's getting eaten, too."

As the day grew longer, Fawn began to agree with Stacy's prediction. The mosquitoes were just horrible, and at first the two girls tried to keep walking fast, hoping that the irritating insects couldn't land on a moving target. But that didn't work, and soon their hands and arms were in constant motion, trying to keep the horrible, buzzing bloodsuckers away from them.

When they got back to camp they found that Mattie had been having the same problem. In fact, she had retreated inside her tent for shelter. Stacy and Fawn did the same, diving into their tent and sealing it shut.

"Oh no," Stacy cried, seeing a few of the pesky little creatures buzzing around inside their tent. "It's bugged in here, too!"

And so, for the next few minutes, she and Fawn went on a search-and-destroy mission for every mosquito that had slipped in through the tent's open flap. Finally, when their tent was apparently bug-free, the two girls spread insect repellent over every inch of their exposed skin.

"This is ridiculous," Stacy said, rubbing some repellent on her ankles. "I smell like an exterminator."

"Phew!" Fawn agreed. "I don't know what's worse—the bug cream or the bugs!" She peered outside. "Wow!" she exclaimed. "Check it out!"

Stacy climbed over her friend to look through the mesh door of the tent. Outside, she could see what seemed like hundreds of the horrible insects circling around the campsite.

"Hey, mosquito expert," Mattie called from her tent, "what do you suggest we do now?"

Stacy looked at Fawn. "Well? You *are* the expert."

Fawn shrugged. "I don't know," she said defensively. "The females need blood in order to produce their eggs. I'm afraid they'll stay around as long as we do."

Stacy looked worried. "How do they know we're still here?"

"Lots of different ways," Fawn said. "The heat coming off of our bodies, the way we smell—maybe they can even tell we're here by the carbon dioxide in our breath."

"What?" demanded Mattie. "Talk louder. If I'm going to be eaten alive, I want to know why."

"I read somewhere that by following the carbon dioxide in the air, a mosquito can track the breath of a sleeping person back to its source," Fawn said, raising her voice.

"What does that have to do with anything?" asked Stacy, getting a little annoyed with Fawn, the Mosquito Woman.

"What she's saying," Mattie concluded, "is that they're hungry, they know we're here, and they won't go away."

Fawn bit her lip. "Uh, yeah. That pretty much sums it up."

Stacy stared outside the tent door. It seemed the swarm had gotten bigger since they had taken cover inside. This just figures, she thought bitterly. *Wade and his stupid friends probably don't have a single mosquito bugging them.* "Look, you guys," she said, "I want to camp out, but I don't want to spend the whole time trapped inside this tent."

"So, what are you saying?" asked Mattie.

Stacy looked at Fawn, who nodded knowingly. "Let's go home," they said in unison.

"Your command is my wish," Mattie agreed from her tent. "Slather yourselves with another layer of repellent and let's pack up!"

A few minutes after stepping out of their tent, Stacy realized she'd made a wise decision. The mosquitoes must have numbered in the thousands. And although the repellent seemed to make them hesitate, it didn't stop all of them. Squeaking in pain, the girls packed the tents as best they could while they danced around, slapping mosquitoes dead by the dozens. When they were just about packed up, Mattie yelled, "Forget the rest! Let's get out of here!" And with that, she broke into a run out of the campsite with Stacy and Fawn close behind.

At first it seemed as if the mosquitoes had been left behind by the sudden departure, and the three girls slowed down to a quick walk along the trail. But within minutes the swarm had found them again.

"This is horrible!" Fawn cried as the tiny, blood-bloated bodies buzzed around her.

"Let's try another way," suggested Mattie, her hands waving like a fan in front of her face. "Maybe this trail goes through a wet patch or something. Maybe that's why they're so thick here." She struck off to one side, with Stacy and Fawn right on her heels.

For a moment, it seemed that Mattie had guessed correctly, for the thick cloud of insects faded away to an almost bearable level.

"That was incredible," Stacy gasped, looking behind them. "We're going to itch for a month."

"And you mean to tell me those were all females?" Mattie asked her sister in disbelief.

Fawn nodded. "I think so. And it looks like this year the problem is even worse."

Suddenly, as if punctuating Fawn's sentence, an enormous swarm of the hideous insects descended on them again. This time the cloud of bugs was even thicker than before. What was worse, the repellent seemed to have worn off. In seconds, the mosquitoes covered them like a blanket of bugs, and soon the three girls looked more like three shambling mounds of tiny, black bodies than they did like human beings.

Fawn finally had to close her eyes in order to protect them and was forced to stop walking. All she could hear was the whine of thousands of wings in her ears. "Mattie!" she screamed. "What should—"

But Fawn couldn't finish her sentence. For after finding fresh, new territory suddenly opened to them, the mosquitoes swarmed into the horrified girl's mouth.

Mattie, who had heard her sister scream, knew better than to open her mouth. She whipped the winged bodies off her face with a sweep of her hand and managed to clear her vision enough to see a shape lying on the ground next to her, a shape that was her sister. *Run!* Mattie's brain screamed at her as she felt millions of tiny pinpricks stabbing into her flesh, each one carrying away a little more of her life. But it was too late to run. For even as Mattie's brain told her legs to move, she, too, was collapsing to the ground while the hungry mosquitoes continued to feed.

Stacy also heard Fawn's scream and the choking sound her friend made as she tried to breathe through the mass of tiny bodies in her mouth. Then she thought she heard a thud, as if a body had fallen to the ground. Powered by terror, and blinded by a layer of mosquitoes, Stacy managed to take off as fast as her mosquito-covered legs would carry her.

Miraculously, she didn't fall. Even more miraculous was the fact that she seemed to have left the mosquitoes

behind. Rubbing her hands over her face, trying to clear her vision, she raced on—not caring where she was going as long as it was away from those horrible bugs.

Finally, running out of breath, Stacy came to an abrupt halt at the edge of a marshy pond. She had no idea how long she had been running, but she knew her lungs would burst if she took another step. Falling to her knees, she sucked air into her chest in ragged gasps.

She tried to tell herself that her friends were all right, but she knew they were probably dead. Despondent, she burst into tears.

"I'll get you," Stacy cried. "I'll get every last one of you for killing my friends. I'll make sure every inch of this land is covered with poison!"

As the sobs tore from Stacy's throat, they masked the approach of the creature rising out of the scum-covered water behind her. But gradually, as the drone of its gigantic wings grew louder, Stacy became aware of its huge presence. Almost too terrified to move, she slowly turned around to face the pond behind her.

There, as big as a helicopter, was a tremendous mosquito hovering over the water. Its abdomen was grossly swollen with what Stacy was certain was another generation of offspring, a whole generation that their monster queen mother would want to feed with an enormous amount of blood.

As Stacy slowly rose, willing her legs to make a terrified run for her life, the beating of the giant mosquito's wings bent the marsh grass down, uncovering a final horror for Stacy's eyes.

She had been wrong—Wade and his friends *had* been bugged by the mosquitoes. As she stared at the shriveled body of her brother—now completely sucked dry of blood—Stacy's heart began to beat wildly. Frantic, she looked around her for an escape route . . . and then the mosquito descended on its next meal.

THE END

Just Deserts

$\mathscr{S}$LOWLY EVAN'S THOUGHTS CRAWLED BACK into his head. He tried to open his eyes, but for some reason, the lid of his right eye seemed to be stuck. And his right shoulder hurt, too—*really* hurt. As his awareness grew, he realized he was curled into a ball and wedged against something hard, yet soft at the same time.

Where am I? he wondered.

It was silent—somehow *too* silent. Forcing his right eye open with his fingertips, Evan saw that he was inside the cabin of a small plane, the front nose of which was buried in the ground. The Plexiglas window was cracked all the way across, but was still in its frame.

"I've been in a plane crash," Evan whispered in awe, blinking to clear his blurry vision. He peered outside a tiny window of the wreckage. *Where am I?* he wondered, looking at what appeared to be nothing but a vast desert.

As his eyes refocused, Evan saw that the plane rested on a slant, tilting to the pilot's side—and the pilot was grotesquely wrapped around the steering wheel.

"Dad!" he cried, as things suddenly started coming back to him. "Are you—" But he didn't have to finish his sentence. He could see that his father was dead.

Falling back in shock, Evan's face erupted into tears. Then he realized that he was leaning against the back of the passenger seat. *Where was his mother?* his mind raced. *Had she been in the plane, too?* With another sickening rush of memory, Evan could hear her scolding his dad for not wearing his seat belt. And then he knew for certain that, yes, she too had been with them.

Wrenching himself free of the strap around his waist, Evan squirmed between the two front seats, wincing at the pain from his near-useless right shoulder. He gasped when he saw his mother's body. She was slumped over, with only her seat belt holding her in place. He could see now that her seat had come loose and had slid forward—whether from the impact of the crash or due to Evan's seat slamming into it, he couldn't say. But the question now was, was she alive?

Coming to grips with the horror of what he was seeing, Evan bent down and examined his mother. "Mom?" he croaked, patting her gently.

She was still breathing, but she didn't respond.

"Mom!" he said louder. "Can you hear me?"

When he still got no response, Evan leaned across his mother and pushed at the door handle. But this effort was too much for him, and his head started to spin, followed by a dull throb that pounded in his right temple. Afraid he might faint, he sat back for a moment to think.

The frame of the plane was clearly warped and had caused the door to bend out of alignment. He needed to be where his mother was in order to push with all his force on the stuck door. Resolving himself to tackle the task at hand, he wiped away his tears, then carefully worked his mother free of her belt and laid her as gently as he could to one side. Then he propped himself on her seat and hammered at the door with his feet. With a screech of protest, the door finally wrenched open, and Evan slid out of the plane.

Standing on the dusty, parched floor of a shallow gully, Evan nearly fainted, his vision spinning crazily. He staggered over to the side of the plane, then sank to the ground, his head in his hands. "What the . . . ?" he murmured, feeling something sticky in his hair. He looked at his hand and saw that it was covered with blood. It was the final straw for Evan's already battered mind, and he fainted.

𖤘 𖤘 𖤘

Some time later—he wasn't sure when—Evan woke up to searing heat. His first thought was that the plane was on fire, and he quickly rolled to one side and peered at the wreckage.

But there was no fire, and Evan soon realized that what he had felt was the desert sun, hot as a raging fire, beating down on him. He had no idea how long he had lain there, but he did remember that he had originally knelt in the shade when he had gotten out of the plane. Now there was no shade at all.

Feeling slightly nauseated, Evan lurched to his feet and staggered over to the plane to see if his mom had regained consciousness. She was still lying in the same position he had left her in . . . but was no longer breathing.

"No!" Evan screamed, falling over his mother's lifeless body. In horror, he realized that he was suddenly without parents, without help . . . and totally alone.

＊＊＊

That had been yesterday. Now it was morning and he sat in the backseat of the wrecked plane, where he had spent the night. His emotions were gone—baked away by the sun, then frozen during the incredibly cold night. Now he felt nothing—not even sadness at the fact that his parents were dead, not even shock. All he felt was an odd, selfish satisfaction that he alone had survived.

"Now what?" he asked himself in a hoarse whisper. His shoulder and head still ached. If he moved too quickly, he was sure he would faint. And he was hungry, too—but that was nothing compared to the thirst that seemed to suck the moisture from the walls of his throat.

The way Evan figured it, he had two choices: He could try to find help, or he could wait for help to come to him. Slowly he bent forward and studied the instrument panel. It was smashed beyond use, so he wouldn't be able to radio for help. And he had no idea how long it would take for someone to realize the plane was missing. *It could be hours before they find me*, he thought, beginning to panic. *Or days!*

On the other hand, the idea of crossing the arid landscape, which stretched as far as he could see, was a terrifying one. He could probably walk in the direction the plane had been headed, but he had no idea how far it was to civilization. It could be close by, or it could be unreachable.

"I don't want to die," he whimpered, feeling a tear roll down his cheek. Then he burst out into hysterical laughter. He hadn't thought there was even that much water left in his body.

Needing to do something to keep his mind off his situation, Evan searched the interior of the plane. He didn't know what he might find in the way of emergency supplies, but he remembered enough to know that his dad, a very methodical man, would have been prepared for any situation. There had to be something in the plane that could help him—there just *had* to be.

In a compartment behind his seat, Evan found a small canvas bag. Feeling hopeful for the first time, he yanked it out of the storage space and unzipped it to find a first aid kit, a flare gun, matches, a few cans of food, and some shiny foil packages marked "Emergency Water."

"I knew you wouldn't let me down, Dad," Evan exclaimed as he tore open one of the packages and gulped down the warm, metallic-tasting liquid. Then he eagerly opened one of the cans only to find hard, dry biscuits. Shrugging, he stuffed a few into his mouth. Although they were tasteless, they sure were better than nothing.

Feeling slightly energized, Evan contemplated his meager rations. There were four more packets of water and two more cans of biscuits. The first aid kit was all but useless to him, since he couldn't see his head wound anyway, and his shoulder couldn't be helped by bandaging. The flare gun would surely be useful if he could figure out how it worked, and the matches might be handy if he actually found some wood to light a fire.

Stay or go? he asked himself, sitting in the warming interior of the plane as the day grew hotter and hotter.

In the end, it was the heat that made the decision for him. It had increased so rapidly that he figured he'd fry to death if he stayed inside the plane. So, grabbing the canvas bag, Evan eased himself past the stiff forms of his parents, trying not to look at them, and dropped to the ground outside. He knew it was madness to start walking during the daylight hours, so he dug into the cool, sandy soil in the shadow of the plane and waited for the sun to set.

Dozing on and off throughout the blistering hot day, Evan woke only long enough to move out of the sunlight when it crept around the body of the plane to shine on him. Then he had to fight with himself not to drink too much from the water packets, giving in only when his throat was so dry he could hardly swallow.

Later that day, as the sun set, Evan began to get ready to set out. *There's nothing to be afraid of,* he told himself over and over again. *There can't be any big animals out there. What would they survive on?*

Finishing a half-full packet of water and glancing back one last time at the wreckage that contained his parents, Evan set off into the longest night of his life.

᠅ ᠅ ᠅

Although he thought he was well rested, Evan's strength seemed to fade rapidly as he plodded along. The sky was clear and the moon was bright, but he still managed to stumble over unseen rocks and low, thorny bushes. His head pounding and his shoulder throbbing, Evan felt searing pain with each step he took. And when he stopped, the cold desert air started him shivering. The only good note was that, when he could no longer make his legs move, he sank to the ground and was so exhausted that he instantly fell asleep.

But the blinding sun woke him up in what seemed like minutes. Opening his bleary eyes, Evan stared in dismay at the miles of sand that surrounded him without a break.

I've got to get out of this heat, he reasoned, shading his eyes and studying the flat, parched land. Dejected, he sank back to the ground and opened a can of the horribly dry biscuits. He munched on one between sips from his precious package of water and considered his position. The only promise of shelter lay ahead of him, where it looked like there was some sort of dip in the ground. He thought he could see the shape of a large tree there that he could rest under. Pushing himself to move on before the heat of the day set in, Evan started walking.

His vision was a bit better this morning, and soon he was close enough to see that he was approaching another dried-out wash like the one the plane had crashed into. He also saw something else, something that chilled him to the bone despite the unrelenting heat of the morning sun.

There, a little bit before the rim of the gully, was a large path of torn earth that ended at the object he had thought was a tree. Only now he saw what the object truly was—the tail of a plane that lay nose-first in a dry riverbed.

I can't have come full circle! he told himself harshly. *It has to be some other plane.*

Breaking into a stumbling run, Evan made his way to the wreck. Before long, he saw what he feared most—it was the same plane, the one that held his dead parents.

Falling to his knees, Evan burst into bitter tears. "The sun set on my right and when I woke up it was on my left," he mumbled to himself like a madman. "I just *couldn't* have walked in a circle. I slept in the same position all night."

But the evidence was there in front of him. He didn't even have to go near the plane to know it was the same one. The smell of death was so thick in the air around the crash, he almost fell over. *I wasted my strength, my rations, on a giant circle!* his mind screamed. *But how?*

Depression settled over him like a shroud, and he sat for a long while, oblivious to his surroundings. Finally Evan made a decision.

"If I can't tell where I'm going at night," he said out loud, "then I'll have to travel by day." And with that, he set off immediately, trying to keep as relaxed a pace as he could. "I'll just take it easy," he told himself, "and I won't push myself too hard." And so, fixing his eyes on a point on the horizon, Evan began walking toward it . . . and walking . . . and walking . . . and walking.

But travel by day was clearly next to impossible. As hard as Evan tried, he couldn't keep his hands off the water. He drained the rest of the open container, and then another full one. Finally he was too exhausted to think properly and had to stop to rest. Trying to escape the relentless sun, he crawled headfirst into a scraggly bush where he immediately passed out into a deep sleep.

When he woke in the late afternoon, he was pleased to see that the sun was setting directly to his right. "I haven't lost my way *this* time," he congratulated himself, almost giddy with his success.

But his happiness disappeared as soon as he shook out his provisions bag and saw that he was already down to his last packet of water. Trying not to think about what would happen when it was gone, he opened the container and took a sip. Then he got to his feet and started walking.

The sun sank closer to the ground on his right, and as the sky turned violet, an unmistakable shape formed on the horizon. Evan's mouth dropped open, and his brain tried to reject what he was seeing.

It was the tail of a small plane, sticking into the sky at an angle as if it had its nose buried in a ditch. *No,* Evan thought numbly, *this time, it's just not possible!*

Moving almost robotically, his mind teetering on the brink of madness, Evan approached the thing. With each step closer, fear knotted itself more tightly around his heart. Soon he saw the rim of a gully. There, once again, starting a little bit before the rim of the gully, was that same large path of torn earth that ended at the same plane—nose-down in the dirt.

"What's happening to me?" Evan whispered, dropping to his knees. And suddenly an image jumped into his head. It was his dad, fighting to level out the plane. The image was so vivid he could almost hear the panic in his parents' voices as the plane dropped to earth.

"I don't understand it," his father was saying in a strained voice. "There must be some kind of leak in the fuel tank. The gauge is on empty."

Evan's mother wasn't saying anything. Her wide eyes stared from her white face at the ground rushing closer and closer.

"What is *wrong* with me?!" Evan screamed as a final image came into his mind. He and his parents were at the airport, checking out the plane before taking off. Evan hadn't wanted to go on the trip. He'd wanted to stay and go on a camping trip with his friends. But his father had insisted, saying the family didn't spend enough time together. "Now, go check the gas tanks," his father had said sternly, "and quit acting like a spoiled brat."

Evan remembered stomping off, sullenly climbing up on the overhead wing, and yanking off the gas cap. "Fine," he had mumbled, "the tank's full." Then he had slammed the cap back on, not even bothering to give it that crucial turn that would lock it in place.

"Did you make sure to screw the cap on tightly when you replaced it?" his father had asked him when Evan had reported that the tank was full.

Still pouting and feeling mean, Evan had snapped, "Of course I did!"

But now, his guilty conscience would no longer let him lie to the memory of his father. In fact, now Evan realized with dread, his guilty conscience would never let him forget that *he* had caused his parents' death. For his guilt was so strong that it would bring him back to this scene again and again . . . for the rest of his tormented life.

THE END